Richard Dee is a native of Brixham in Devon, England. He left Devon when he was in his teens and settled in Kent. Leaving school at 16 he briefly worked in a supermarket, then went to sea and travelled the world in the Merchant Navy, qualifying as a Master Mariner in 1986

Coming ashore to be with his growing family, he used his sea-going knowledge in several jobs, including Marine Insurance Surveyor and Dockmaster at Tilbury, before becoming a Port Control Officer in Sheerness and then at the Thames Barrier in Woolwich.

In 1994 he was head-hunted and offered a job as a Thames Estuary Pilot. In 1999 he transferred to the Thames River Pilots, where he regularly took vessels of all sizes through the Thames Barrier and upriver as far as HMS *Belfast* and through Tower Bridge. In all, he piloted over 3,500 vessels in a 22-year career with the Port of London Authority.

Richard is married with three adult children and two grandchildren.

His first science-fiction novel *Freefall* was published in 2013, followed by *Ribbonworld* in 2015. September 2016 saw the publication of his Steampunk adventure *The Rocks of Aserol* and *Flash Fiction*, a collection of Short Stories. *Myra*, the prequel to *Freefall*, was published in 2017. He contributed a story to the *1066 Turned Upside Down* collection and is currently working on prequels, sequels, and new projects.

Andorra Pett

and the

Oort Cloud Café

Richard Dee

4Star Scifi

©Richard Dee 2016

All rights reserved.

Published in 2017 by 4Star Scifi

4Star Scifi, Brixham, Devon, England

www.richarddeescifi.co.uk/4Star

I.S.B.N. 978-0-9954581-6-1 (Paperback)

978-0-9954581-5-4 (eBook)

Copyright © Richard Dee 2016

Cover by 4Star Scifi, Matthew Britton and Avalon Graphics

For Yvonne

Chapter 1

"Is that it?"

The entrance was in partial darkness, the alleyway behind me dimly lit with flickering tubes. My heels had clicked on the floor as I passed small piles of rubbish and stained brick-effect cladding. The heels didn't really work here but I was out of my depth and struggling to catch up. Same as the clothes, my designer suit was a little out of place in this riot of grey. It was a splash of colour in a drab working world.

"People don't come down here much," explained my guide, the rental agent for the place I wanted to see. I'd forgotten his name and instead thought of him as Mr Greasy. It suited him, his hair was greasy, as were his clothes; even his smile was up there on the grease-o-meter. He probably thought of himself as a ladies' man, I know we were out on the fringes but surely not? Maybe a desperate ladies' man but I wasn't desperate. At least, not that desperate. Not yet.

Mr Greasy was still talking. "No-one comes down here much since the new diner opened up."

I knew where he meant; we had passed it on the way here, next to a pharmacy and a few other shops. The diner looked new, all gleaming chrome and fresh baked aroma. The barista was archetypal, white teeth and blonde hair, a role model for Mr G. Maybe someone would tell him.

He opened the control box and pressed a few buttons on a keypad. The steel security curtain rolled up to reveal a wide window and a door at the side. Faded lettering proclaimed that this was the 'ucky Strike Bar and Grill'. The 'L' had fallen off; there was the faint outline of where it had been. As the mesh rose, dust fell from the links; the place must have been shut for a while.

"What happened to the last owner?"

"There was a change in the law, no booze allowed any more. It kind of stopped him in his tracks. He gave up and walked away, owes me a month's rent too," said Mr G as he opened the door, this one had a combination lock. He flicked the light switch; dim red lighting came on, just enough to see tables, chairs and a bar. Everything was covered in dust, there were dirty glasses on the tables and the overhead video screens were blank and cobwebbed. That meant spiders, space spiders! I shuddered, I don't like spiders.

"The kitchen is out back, together with stores and living space," continued the sales patter, "a nice master bedroom, en suite." He leered, "Plenty of room for a little lady like yourself. I'll show you."

"Take your word for it," I answered, not wanting to be in a confined space with him; his breath was probably greasy and, well, I didn't want to know about his hands. "Are the fittings and stock all included?"

"All the alcohol's been impounded but everything that's here is yours for two hundred a month, one month up front." I had a sudden feeling, like this place was where I was meant to be.

"I'll take it." OK, so it wasn't ideal but to be honest, I was fed up with running. I'd ignored my feelings before and look where that had got me. I might even grow to like the place. Besides, there wasn't anywhere further to run. We were on the edge of civilisation.

"What you gonna do with it? You can't open it as a bar and we've already got a diner." It was a fair question, I didn't really know but I wasn't going to tell him that.

He moved closer. "Let's seal the deal then," he suggested, with a wink.

One of the advantages of being a short shrimp, as my mother used to say, was that you didn't have to reach down too far to do a man serious damage. I was just contemplating that when he was saved by the arrival of Cy, my friend and business partner, dragging a trolley full of luggage.

"You lost me, Andi," he puffed. "It's bloody dark down here, is this it?"

Greasy backed off; Cy was larger and less greasy than him. He didn't know but Cy had no interest in me in that sort of way. Dave was the love of his life, he had left him to look after me, and that made me feel alternately good and bad, they had seemed as happy together as Trevor and I had.

"He'll wait," Cy had explained on the trip out. "And if he doesn't then I can cry into my cappuccino for a while and move on."

"Pay the man, Cy." I had decided. "Four hundred and let's get the gingham bunting out."

Greasy shook his head. "Gingham! What the hell are you going to do to the place?"

"Maybe the diner needs a little competition," I ventured; this brought a smirk and a shake of the head.

"Mr Munro won't like it."

"Mr Munro can lump it. Shall I tell him or will you?"

He was saved from having to answer by the sight of the money in Cy's hand. He took the notes, counted them and walked away, chuckling in a greasy sort of way. "I'll give you a month," he shouted over his shoulder. I thought that wasn't too much of an endorsement, considering I'd paid for a month. Or maybe that was what he meant.

"You're not serious are you?" said Cy as I walked around the tables to the far wall. "We can't run a café."

I stopped and turned back to him.

"Why not, Cy? It's perfect; remember what that bloke said on the shuttle. There's only one other place selling leisure here, all we have to do is pretend it's the shop in London, just coffee and cake instead of clothes."

"Can you bake cakes, Andi?" He had a point; he'd tried my sandwiches once. He reckoned that I wouldn't be able to do toast without a recipe and a video. I'd show him.

"Yes," I said with confidence, and then I thought about it, "No… sort of; how hard can it be?" My mum had taught me and she'd never killed anyone.

I turned back and continued to the end wall. I had thought the place was dark, I was about to find out if I could make it lighter.

I had spotted the control for the picture windows all along one wall, reaching over the stained bench seats I grabbed it and turned it. The switch was sticky and resisted but in the end it rotated and with a whir the view was revealed as the shutters went up.

Saturn's rings in all their glory filled the room with reflected light, the space opened out and the room became more than just a derelict and unloved bar. Even an 'ucky' one.

This was now my café, and I was going to make it work. I'd even thought of a name. And Cy was going to help me.

"Welcome to the Oort Cloud Café, Cy."

He shook his head. "I just hope you know what you're doing."

It's about time I introduced myself, I'm Andorra Pett, my friends all call me Andi. I'm short and feisty with a few curves and a mess of dark hair. I used to run a vintage clothes shop back on Earth when I was young and still believed in happy ever after. Then there was Trevor, he said I was the love of his life, I believed him too, right up to the moment that I caught him with my soon-to-be-ex best friend Masie. Then I knew it was time to change everything. I raided the accounts, took the money and ran. That was a bit out of character for me, I wasn't a space hound or even the flying to Spain type.

But, I thought, it's time to get over it and DO something. Cy, short for Cyril – and don't laugh – caught up with me and tried to stop me at the port but he ended up coming with me. He said he was looking out for me but I reckoned he wanted a break, the same as I did. Why else would he try to stop me with a suitcase of his own? Cy was my assistant from the shop, a genius with a sewing machine and my confidant. Plus he tended to bail me out when my mouth got me into trouble.

"Won't you miss Dave?" I asked as we boarded the shuttle up to the orbiting ship, ahead was Mars, then here.

"Maybe," Cy answered. "But then I've always wanted adventure. Keeping you safe should guarantee me that."

Chapter 2

Next morning I woke up with a pain in my back. I was laying on two of the long seat cushions from the sofas in the café, side by side with a third cushion for a pillow, all covered with a sheet. I had found a reasonably clean duvet, minus cover, and a towel in the bedroom. The old mattress was skip fodder. At least my feet weren't cold.

I went to the bathroom and splashed a little water around. The tap ran brown for a few seconds as all the rust washed through. It was one of those taps where the flow stopped if you didn't push on top of it. I hate them. Maybe there was a water shortage.

Then I remembered, I was on a *space station*, duh! Of course there was a water shortage. My hair was a mess, it needed a wash and had gone all 'been to bed' on me. No need to bother too much with that, I would be cleaning all day. I just tied it up; it wasn't like I'd be seeing anyone at this hour. I looked at my watch; it was 8 a.m. station time, would anybody expect me to be open for coffee yet? Would they even know that I was here?

I couldn't find a plug so I couldn't fill the basin. I washed, sort of, and dragged on jeans and a tee, put on my pumps and wandered through the rooms checking them out. I'd been so tired the night before that I hadn't bothered. I'd tried to open the wardrobe door and it had fallen off. I took that as a message, have a sleep, Andi, it had said. So I did.

There were two more bedrooms. One could be for Cy, the other seemed to have been used as a store and gym. I could see all sorts of very dusty exercise equipment, a cross trainer, rowing machine and some weights in a rack, plus a few bits of random twisted metal. And there was a clean mattress on the bed; still in its plastic bag. That would be coming my way, once I'd got organised.

Then there was a lounge and a small kitchen as well as another bathroom. Plenty of space for me and Cy, once we had got ourselves sorted. And no curtains, only bland roller blinds at the round windows. Weren't they called portholes? Whatever; at least we shouldn't have people peering in at us from outside.

The view was pretty spectacular though, I could see Saturn's rings and amazingly enough they weren't solid like you would expect from the way you see them in books. Close up, they were made of millions of rocks all moving about in a random pattern while following a circular path around the planet. And even more amazing was the number of small craft I could see, there were all colours, bright yellow, green and purple. They looked like flying bulldozers and cranes with flashes of red from their engines as they roamed amongst the rocks, they must be the miners. They would probably be too busy mining to come in for a peek at my porthole. It looked decidedly dangerous. You wouldn't catch me out in one of those!

Retracing my steps past my bedroom, I passed the entrance to the café; it led in behind the counter. The corridor continued to another set of rooms, I looked out towards Cy; I could locate him in the gloom by the sound. He was snoring loudly; flat out on his back and dressed to kill in his paisley boxers. He hadn't cared about finding a bed, he'd just dragged cushions onto the floor and being a bloke wasn't bothered about snuggling under sheets or quilts either.

He sounded like some sort of sea creature, the kind that holds its breath for half an hour and then lets it all out in one. Except he was doing it every five seconds; Dave must have been deaf. Mind you, Cy looked fit enough, fitter than Trevor had ever looked. The thought of Trevor soured the enjoyment I felt at being as far away from him as it was possible to be and still be civilised.

It suddenly hit me, this was all mine. Well, technically I suppose it was all ours. And I had to make it work. I had to get Cy onside. It seemed overwhelming for a second; I remembered that the clothes shop had felt the same on the first day and that had turned out alright. What could possibly go wrong?

I carried on with my inspection and found a bigger kitchen, well fitted out with a serving hatch to the space behind the bar, a proper washroom with laundry machines and more of the stupid taps, far too much cleaning gear for my liking and two storerooms. The dry store had rows of shelving with bags of coffee, flour and various other things. A lot of the stuff was out of reach; well, the top shelves were over five-feet-two above ground. I would need to find a box to stand on to see what was up there. Cy could do that, I might get nosebleed.

The last room had two glass fronted fridges which were working but were filled with a fine selection of mouldy and sure-to-be-smelly foodstuffs. I left them closed. There would be nothing for breakfast in there. There were also two enormous chest freezers. One was empty and open, the other was locked but according to the panel was full and at minus eighteen degrees. And in the corner, there was the missing letter 'L', propped up and dusty, it must have been there for a while.

"That you, Andi?" Cy called from the café. He had woken up, it was a bit early for him, it must be space lag.

"I'm in the back," I replied. "Are you decent?"

"Never, but the nearest thing you'll probably get to it on this dump."

Oh dear, he sounded like he was in grumpy mode. He didn't want to be here, I'd better be nice. "I'm just checking out the stores, get your trousers on please, it's far too early for temptation."

He laughed, "Yours or mine?" Then there was the dramatic pause. "No, definitely not mine." I'd heard that so many times I didn't bother answering; there was no point in encouraging him. Let him wake up and get his face on first. And after a coffee, he would be happier. At least I could make him a coffee. I ought to be able to; I was in a café after all.

There was a swish as he flounced down the alleyway towards the bathroom, dragging his suitcase. On past performance, I knew that he would be a good hour making himself presentable. There didn't seem to be any point in waiting, it was time to open the shutters and face the day. I shut the lid on the empty freezer and turned it on to full. We would need it for stock; I might as well get it cooled down ready.

Walking back into the space behind the bar, I saw the coffee machine; it was dusty like everything else but the same as the one they had in the shop across the road from us in London. I got coffee from them every morning and I could remember how Chaz used to make it. I checked the water was connected and turned it on. The red light winked at me and it rumbled a bit.

I left it to have a think while it woke itself up and turned the lights on. I walked over to the door, avoiding all the table corners and Cy's bed, and pressed the button for the shutters. The motor spluttered into life. As the steel barrier rose I saw feet, several of them; outside the doorway.

So much for nobody noticing. News must travel fast in this place, there can't have been much else to interest the population, a crazy lady renting the derelict bar must have been pure gossip gold, and after all, how many times could you say "Saturn's looking nice today"?

I opened the door. "Good morning," I said and they nodded in reply, looking me up and down in a way that I found slightly annoying.

There were three of them, a delegation maybe. Two were identikit blondes, the sort that had made me feel so inadequate back in London. Tall and pencil thin with the same bleached bob and fitted boiler suits they made the third seem out of place. She was shorter and rounder, almost a normal shape in fact. Her head was shaved and there were multiple tattoos visible on her arms and legs. She wore a vest and shorts, large boots and rolled down socks. A tool belt hung from her waist. She seemed to be the spokesperson. "Hi," she said, putting out a hand like a bunch of bananas. I took it; her grip was strong, almost masculine. "I'm Tina."

She certainly was, it said so on her arm. Several times. Perhaps she was forgetful?

"These two are Lou and Terri." The blondes nodded. They looked around at the bar.

"We haven't been in here for ages," one said.

"Ages," echoed the other.

"It's dusty," said one.

"Very dusty," agreed the other.

"Don't mind them," said Tina. "They're two separate people; honestly."

"Tina," they both said at once, giggling, "naughty!"

"Can we come in?" asked Tina. "We are in serious need of caffeine and we heard that you were opening up today."

I didn't know where they had got that from but what the hell; I might as well start at the deep end.

"And we bought you breakfast," said blonde one, brandishing a box. "We made you both a few things." So they knew there were two of us, if they got that then the station's rumour mill was definitely in good working order.

"Home-made things, not crap from the diner," added blonde number two. That was bribery, but I was hungry. I stepped aside.

"The diner won't let Tina in," said blonde one. "She's banned."

"Forever," nodded blonde two. "We're not," she added proudly, "because we're not rude like her."

"But we don't like drinking in there on our own," said number one.

"Tina's fun and Munro's a bastard!" agreed the other one. Not only did they look the same, they both sounded the same; this was going to be hard to keep up with. What was their job here? Were they the cabaret?

They all came in and sat at one of the cleaner tables. "I'll go and

16

find the coffee," I said.

Blonde number two stood back up. "I'll show you," she offered. "I used to work here, till Mike's hands wandered too far, I know where everything is." I hoped that she just meant the controls on the coffee machine.

She could be useful. "Do you want a job?" I asked her. "Oh yes please," she squealed. "And Lou would too, wouldn't you, Lou?" So this one must be Terri.

"Yes please," said her blonde echo, Lou. "I missed out on the wandering hands." She sounded upset; perhaps I ought to introduce her to Mr Greasy, if she hadn't already had the pleasure. "I bought milk as well." She held up a container. "If there's any still in the fridge it'll be growing things by now."

Cy chose that moment to make his entrance, he had rushed; he must have heard the women's voices. Even though he wouldn't be interested in them in the way they thought, they might not know that to start with. It all depended on whether he was in full camp mode or not. And he was handsome enough to intrigue them, he had that undefinable allure. He just loved to be around women. It was such a waste. They would be eating out of his hand in no time.

Chapter 3

"Hello," both blondes said in appreciative unison, their voices rising slightly at the last "o". Tina just looked at him; she had realised straight away what the other two had missed. Maybe it was the batik shirt, one of his migraine inducing ones.

Cy as usual had spotted the person that interested him the most and had made a bee-line. This only served to make the other two more determined to monopolise him. Really, it was so obvious that I could have sold tickets. There would be disappointment; tears before solitary bedtime.

"Hi," said Cy to Tina. "I'm Cy, you alright?"

"Yeah," she replied, ignoring the blondes circling around like a couple of skinny sharks.

"What's your job on this bloody place then?" he asked.

"I'm a welder for the Scooper squad."

Cy looked all innocent. "You must have some big dogs on the station?" he said, straight-faced. He paused for effect, "If the scoops need *welding*?"

Tina roared with laughter and slapped him on the back. "You're alright," she announced. "Good sense of humour. And timing. I like you." They went into a huddle and you'd think they'd been friends since they had been infants. Which they both still were, in a way.

The blondes gave up trying to attract Cy's attention and actually came back to help me with the coffee, to be fair they knew their way around the bar and kitchen and were very efficient with the kit. Employing them would be a smart move. It wasn't as complicated as I'd thought. After all, I'd watched people make coffee for me enough times; they helped me work the machine and we made the drinks. We carried them over to Cy and Tina, who were sitting on opposite sides of one of the tables. They were arm-wrestling. Tina looked to be winning.

"It's the best out of… about thirty-seven I think," said Cy, probably part of his ingratiating plan. You couldn't help but smile though.

"You sure you're not letting her win?" I asked him. He ignored that.

"Hey, Andi," he said. "Tina here can get us all sorts of stores cheap, she knows someone on the Earth shuttles. She can even get us a day out with the miners on the rings."

"Great," I said with no enthusiasm whatsoever. "Can she open the freezer?"

"Before you do that," said Lou, or it might have been Terri, they had moved and I'd lost track. "Do we really get the job?"

"Can you bake?" asked Cy, they perked up when he actually talked to them.

"Can we bake? Of course we can, best cakes on the station," said one of them. "Try these," she passed him the box.

"Wow," he said. "Look, Andi." Inside on layers of tissue were pan-au-chocolate and some things with raisins, I probably ought to learn the names. They were golden and flaky and smelt divine. Cy bit into one. "Incredible," he mumbled around a mouthful.

"We made them, I told Andi, they're not the part-baked; Vac-Pac rubbish that Munro serves up in the diner," said the other one.

"Do you remember the one we made for the astronomer we didn't like?"

"With the laxative powder in the cocoa?" They both dissolved into giggles. Again.

I tried one and it tasted amazing, they made my efforts seem a bit pathetic. If this was the standard, I needed to up my game. Hopefully I could get these two helping, if they weren't already booked for panto somewhere.

"That's great; these are brilliant and just what we need." I was relieved, perhaps I wouldn't have to inflict too much of my baking on anyone, the laxative one sounded like it would have the same effect as my standard recipe. "But how do we tell you two apart?"

"That's easy, I'm the clever one," said Terri.

"No you're not," said Lou. "I'm the clever one."

Oh help, it was like a bad comedy show on the TV.

"Tell you what," I said desperately. "I'll hire you both, and get you name badges."

That seemed to please them; they actually looked excited at the name badge idea. "We know where Mike kept the freezer key," said one of them; they skipped off, hand in hand.

"What is it with those two?" asked Cy. "I'm exhausted already."

Tina grinned. "You're wondering how I put up with them," she said. "Well, I think that they're the only two genuine people on the station. Both of them are experimental astrophysicists."

She must have seen my face drop. "Seriously, they both have more letters after their names than anyone I've ever met! They work in the observatory, when they feel like it. They're that clever that no-one objects. They don't want anyone to think they're geeks or posh, aloof types and they have a wicked sense of humour."

"They had me fooled," said Cy, he was on his second, or was it third of the pastries. Tina grinned and carried on.

"They play the dumb blonde routine with newcomers and anyone who can't tell them apart. They swap boyfriends mid-date, confuse everyone and generally get up to as much mischief as they think they can get away with. But never with any malice. You'll find that most people have a sneaking admiration for them, even miserable people like Wallis and Munro."

Who was Wallis? I'd heard the name Munro yesterday, Mr G had mentioned it.

"Because they act like they haven't got a clue, like they're in their own world," Tina continued, "people forget themselves and say things in front of them. Treat them right and they'll keep you up to date with everything that's going on."

"Are they twins or just lookalikes?" asked Cy.

"They're twins, Lou has a mole on the side of her face, she's three minutes older than Terri, and plays on the big sister bit; she always tries to talk first."

Before I could ask Tina who Wallis was, or anything else, the twins came back, but they weren't being dumb blondes any more. They both sat stone faced. Now that Tina had mentioned it I spotted the mole on one face.

"Tina," Lou said in a quiet voice, "you remember how Mike was supposed to have just left, owing a month's rent?"

"Yeah," said Tina.

"Wasn't it to do with the alcohol thing?" I added, repeating what Mr G had told me.

"That's right," said Tina. "He just left without anyone seeing him go, I thought it was odd, we all did. Why?"

They looked at each other.

"He never left!"

"He's in the freezer!"

"In some sort of bag!"

Chapter 4

Talk about conversation stoppers. That was right up there with 'your spaceship's got a hole'.

"What!" Cy almost choked on his coffee. "There's a body in the freezer?!"

Tina nodded, as if she wasn't surprised. "Bloody Munro, I might have guessed," she muttered.

Lou and Terri had got over the shock, now they looked pleased with themselves. "We thought it was strange, how no-one saw him go," said one. "No-one," said the other.

The double act was back and it was getting tedious. If they were as clever as Tina reckoned, I might need them to get me out of the mess I had managed to plonk myself in. And I had the sneaking suspicion that I was already in it further than I should be.

"OK you two," I pleaded. "Can we stop the act now and be serious please. I don't know what I've got into here but I could do with a bit of sensible help."

"Sure," said Lou. "It gets exhausting after a while anyway. And that's what we've come to tell you. We overheard Munro talking to one of the control room crew while we were working yesterday evening. He said that he knew someone had taken the lease on this place and that he was going to come over and take a look around. He'll probably be over soon; he's part of the management and as it's his place it makes sense. He'll try and frighten you off, in a nice way of course."

"Who is this Munro that I keep hearing about?" I asked. I remembered that Mr Greasy had said that he wouldn't like my leasing the café. "Can't I just tell him I found it? After all, I only got here yesterday."

There were intakes of breath and worried looks. "Trust us," said Tina. "You don't want to get involved or admit anything; it's possible that Munro put him there, or at least knows who did. Best if you keep quiet."

"Oh, bloody marvellous," said Cy, he was very agitated. "What the hell are we doing here, Andi? Just cos Trev was getting a bit of extracurricular; you've got the hump and we've come all the way out here. Now we're involved with… what, gangsters? There's a body out the back and we're gonna be hiding it. Who is this Munro anyway?"

"He's the big man around here," said Tina. "Unofficially he runs the place."

"He owns the franchise for the diner and some of the retail units, including this one," Lou said. "Officially the mining company own the station, what they say goes but they have a council thing for non-employed residents. They don't want to be distracted from mining with arguments over who's running the café so they leave it up to them."

Oh this just got better.

"Munro's not on the council but he has a lot of influence over them, and with the company that runs the supply shuttles. Basically, he keeps his finger on the pulse, what he says goes, if he doesn't like you or want you around he'll make your life impossible until you get fed up and leave."

And better.

"And he owns the diner?" said Cy. "Our competition, our landlord, do we have to call him Don? Kiss his ring?" That got blank looks from Lou and Terri.

"We don't know his first name," one of them said. "He's just Munro." Tina grinned.

"But would he kill someone?" I was worried, I could be next. Or Cy could. What had we, I, done?

"There's never been a suspicious death on the station before," said Terri. "A bit of light beating and plenty of psychological warfare but no extreme violence, the security guards would stop turning a blind eye if he went too far." That was comforting, maybe.

"There were the suicides," Lou added. "And that bloke who had the coffee stall in the park; a bit dodgy and coincidental if you ask me." She didn't elaborate and I didn't feel like knowing.

"So aren't you asking for trouble just being here with me and not in *his* diner?"

"I have to drink coffee somewhere," said Tina. "And I work for the miners, they're a protective bunch; he can't touch me. Their union, you'll hear it called the guild, well they're a stroppy crowd, if they stop work there's panic. And they love to stop work; it gives them a feeling of power. Anyway, I can't go in the diner in working gear, I have to get takeaway and go to the park. He'll sell me that but I won't buy it on principle."

"Of course he will! It's the same with us," said Terri. "We work for the government, directly under the university on Mars; the observatory is their investment, the space is leased from the miners. So whatever Munro thinks about us, we're fireproof too."

"And we won't go in there on principle either," added Lou. "There are lots of people who make their own coffee and stuff just to show him that he's not the big boss he thinks he is."

Someone had killed the previous owner though, if not him then that was just one off the list. "Who else didn't like Mike, then?"

Lou rolled her eyes. "Loads of people," she said. "First of all, a lot of the miners. They work long hours and it's dangerous out there, they saw him as lazy, and in a soft job. He was always flirting, chasing after their bored wives and girlfriends while they were out risking life and limb. Talk is that he seduced quite a few of them."

"Then of course," continued Terri, "there were the women he had dumped. Because of him, some of them had lost their men, now he didn't want them either. A lot of them just left but the ones who stuck it out had to grovel, and they were resentful and jealous of his latest conquests." As she stopped talking Lou started, they had forgotten their deal and were finishing each other's sentences again.

"Of course no-one really knows which of the women he was sleeping with."

"There are a few who admitted it, a few who left and the rest; well it's a guessing game."

"If you really want to get involved, I could tell you a few things," Tina joined in, her tone suggested that it was the last thing I should do. "I used to hear the miners talking while I was repairing their Scoopers. And before you ask," she looked at Cy, "it scoops rocks from the rings."

He looked pained.

"They're full of useful metals and compounds," Lou added.

"All sorts of rare earths and stuff," agreed Terri. Couldn't they keep on topic?

I heard the door open and even though I had my back to it, from the expression on the girls' faces I just knew that Mr Munro had arrived. I was right. And he was mob-handed.

I turned in my seat; three men came into the bar, in black suits and serious faces. There were two big, dark-bearded hunks and a slightly smaller, blonde haired one; they parted to allow the man himself to enter. He looked around, pulled a sour face, nodded to Tina and the twins. Evidently there was a bad smell in the place; you could almost see it under his nose.

"Good morning, I'm your landlord, Jasper Munro," he said. Not Don then. He was tall, dark and probably considered himself handsome. A fine quality light grey suit hung off his lean frame; sunglasses incongruously perched on cropped hair, so short you couldn't really tell its colour. "I need to do an inspection before you take the lease."

"I've already paid," I said. He looked straight through me. "How could you? There's been no account activity logged."

"I paid cash, two months." What account activity? I didn't have one here. And how would he know that anyway? Then I realised what Tina meant about him running things.

He would know.

He thought for a moment. "Ah yes, but I expect that Mr Wallis neglected to tell you that that was a non-returnable deposit, pending a suitability check."

"Too right he did, Mister," Cy got to his feet and the suits tensed. He was taller and more muscular then Munro but give him his due, he had balls; he never flinched. "Like she said, we paid for two months, in cash."

"No doubt you have a receipt then. Sit down, I'm not arguing with you, just acting like a responsible landlord." His face showed irritation, at least now I knew who Mr G was. Maybe it crossed Munro's mind that he might be on the take.

"I'll remind Mr Wallis to complete the formalities but I need to make sure everything is in order before I let you take over. It's station policy." The two big suits nodded in unison, like a henchman version of Lou and Terri. Blondie was staring at the girls.

Put like that it sounded reasonable, even logical. "Calm down, Cy, we're new here and we don't know how things work." He sat and I put my hand on his.

"You must be Miss Pett," he said to me. "Welcome to the station, I hope your time here will be… pleasant." I heard Tina pretending to be sick, he turned to her.

"Ms Weyth," he said, "if you've drunk the coffee in here then I'm not surprised you feel like that, perhaps the diner would be a more suitable place for you." He paused, playing Cy's timing trick. "But no, you're barred. You'll get used to it here then, with luck."

"Call me Andi," I said, he dragged his attention back to me, an eyebrow raised.

"What is it with you women? You all have male names, why? You're Andi; these two are Lou and Terri. Do you all want to be men?" The burly guards sniggered. The blonde one actually went red, bless him.

There was no answer to that, at least none that tripped off the tongue. Right at this moment I wouldn't have minded being a bloke though. Preferably one with a baseball bat to wipe his smug expression away.

"Excuse me," he said. "I'll have a look round then, don't bother showing me, I know where everything is." After what we had been talking about, I hoped he didn't mean the body. He went behind the bar; turning left he disappeared into the kitchen and stores. Perhaps one of us should have gone with him. Looking at their blank faces, I got the feeling the suits wouldn't have liked the idea. I noticed that they were all carrying some sort of radio; I could see earpieces, the wires coming out of their shirt collars. What did they need them for? Or perhaps they were listening to music and hadn't heard a word.

I wondered if Munro would try to open the freezer. I decided that it would be best not to make any fuss. Beside me, Cy looked the picture of innocence. After a few minutes, we saw him go past, heading for the living quarters, two minutes later he came back. He looked disappointed, as if he had expected to see something that wasn't there. Maybe it was a body?

"It seems alright," he said. "But there's mouldy food in the fridges. As the foodstuffs were part of the price you paid, I'll get them replaced for you; a run-around will be along later. If there's anything else you need, order it and if we haven't got it, it'll be on the next shuttle, they arrive weekly. Go to the commissary on the arrival deck, one of the ladies there will explain how everything works; money, supplies that sort of thing."

"Thank you," I said, I hadn't been expecting that.

"Not at all, Miss, err Andi. I'm not going to be accused of any underhand practices." Or maybe he was just lulling me into a false sense of security.

He wiped at a dusty chair and sat. "Now it's no secret that you will be in competition with me. I'm not enthusiastic about that but I'm a businessman and I suppose that it's healthy to have two places selling the same product. It promotes quality and keeps prices reasonable. Only one will ultimately survive of course but that's just the way it is."

He looked around again; I felt sure he knew more about this Mike person than he was letting on. As he peered around the room I followed his gaze. He took in the dusty and ripped seats, the remains of the last party, glasses and bottles, snack packets. And then his eyes fell on the bar, the beer taps and all the paraphernalia of a drinking man's establishment.

"You have a lot of work to do here, to turn this… place into a café like the diner," he said.

"I don't want to turn it into the diner," I replied. "I want this to be somewhere different."

He laughed. "I don't think there will be any danger of getting the two places mixed up."

"We're helping her," said one of the twins. "And all the people you've pissed off will come in here."

That seemed to amuse him; a grin played around his mouth.

"Maybe. We'll see. I noticed rubbish lying around. It's a hazard and needs proper disposal. I trust that you haven't disposed of any garbage yet?"

His tone was innocent, but there was a questioning depth to it. "There's been no official request received. We must follow procedure on the station; all our lives depend on it. I'm sure you'll get used to it quickly. There'll be a rule book somewhere; these ladies will know most of the important stuff. Please don't think that it's just us being over dramatic or petty, we're in space and it doesn't care if we live or die. Just mind you do things properly and if you're not sure, ask."

He rose. "Good luck in your venture, and may the best man, or at least the one with the best man's name, win. Oh, and the 'L' needs putting back. On the sign. Get an electrician to do it. Unless you want to be forever known as the 'Ucky' café."

"I'm changing the name."

"Are you now," he said. "Let them know in writing and the council will consider it."

He left, followed by the suits. They shut the door behind them.

We all breathed out.

"Smooth operator," Cy opined.

"Never mind that," I said, turning to the twins. "Do you think he saw the body?"

They looked smug; enough teeth were on show to get a dentist excited.

"Oh we moved it; it's stood up at the back of the broom cupboard."

"Behind everything."

My face fell.

"Don't worry, it's frozen solid. We'll get it back in the freezer before it melts too much. It's safe enough now, he won't be back."

"How did you know?" I started.

"We didn't but it was logical," said Lou. "If he knew it was here, he wouldn't want you to find it before he could embarrass you with finding it himself."

"There might be evidence on it," finished Terri.

"Which you've just compromised," added Tina.

"And now he thinks it's not here."

"If it was him that put it here, he's going to be puzzled."

"Or mad."

"OK, OK," I said. "That's enough, one at a time. Let's get him back in the freezer and decide what to do next."

I needed more coffee, lots more.

Chapter 5

We slammed the lid on the corpse, which we had put back face down in the bottom of the empty freezer, the one I had turned on in anticipation of stock. Cy and Tina then piled boxes of burgers and fries over it, hiding the desperate expression and the sheer frostiness of it all. The twins had said that it was in a body bag and I had imagined a fully enclosed zip-up thing. This one had a face plate, more like a spacesuit really. There were blue and black bruises on the neck, enough to suggest the cause of death. I still figured that we ought to go to security but Tina advised against it.

"You don't know how things work here," she said. "You could end up on the wrong end of a murder charge."

"That's stupid," said Cy, "we weren't even here."

"Little details like that have never mattered before. Munro has enough clout to make it stick," Lou dryly commented.

I thought about it. If Munro knew that the body was here, he would want to move it before I found it. Or maybe he just thought that it might be here, in which case he would want to check. Or perhaps he really was just doing the landlord bit. It was confusing, clearly things were different on this artificial world; once again I realised that I was going to have to catch up.

"So, what do we do now then?" asked Cy. "I don't like it here, Andi. I think we should just put it down to experience and move on."

I wasn't having that, I'd set my heart on the Oort Cloud Café. Hell, it even sounded cute. And a little thing like a dead body in the freezer and a few hostile natives were not going to put me off. And I loved the idea of a good mystery, especially if I could stick it to the culprit. Whoever it might turn out to be. Plus, we were four hundred down.

"You wanted adventure, Cy," I reminded him. "I think we need to have a good look around, size up the way things are and make a plan. I want to know more about what we've got ourselves into."

Cy muttered something about 'you've got us into', but that was OK. As long as he wasn't in outward revolt he would have my back. And maybe I should have wondered, what *else* could possibly go wrong?

"I'll get you some more appropriate clothes," said Lou. "You'll need boiler suits and flat shoes; your heels will catch in the plating on the lower decks."

"You don't want to slip and land on your arse," agreed Terri. I had to laugh; falling on my arse was my speciality, it was the only thing I could do with any real guarantee of success.

"How am I going to open this place and get customers?" I wondered out loud.

"Don't worry about that," Terri reassured me. "As well as all the home bakers, there're a lot of people that only drink in the diner cos there's nowhere else to go. Like we said to Munro. We'll help you get this place cleaned up and spread the word; they'll come."

"She's right," Tina announced, draining her coffee. "I'd love to help but I'm afraid I've gotta get back, thanks for the drink, Andi," she said. "The twins will see you right but if you need anything come and find me, my workshop's on the deck below the admin offices. Follow the yellow pathway, anyone'll tell you."

"Thanks, Tina," I replied, meaning it. Yellow pathway; what the hell was that? Some sort of reference to Oz, well I definitely wasn't in Kansas. She stomped out, the tool belt jingling, with Lou and Terri's suggestions that it was convenient, her leaving as the work was about to start, ringing in her ears. Tina just laughed and waved as she left.

"Meanwhile I have a café to open," I said to the twins. "When can you two start work?"

"How about right now?" they said in unison.

"You're hired, both of you."

If they were willing, I might as well get them working. I was a café owner with bills to pay; I needed to make some cash. If we were opening tomorrow I needed help and these two were offering. Lou and Terri were on the staff and between us we had a bit to do.

Chapter 6

We started off by getting rid of all the alcohol related equipment, piling it up in the corner, along with the old mattress from the master bedroom. Then we cleaned everything that was left, including the public washrooms; not a pleasant job. There was a good selection of things to do this with in the cupboard that had been Mike's temporary home and between us we soon had the place dust and dirt free. We would need stuff to repair and re-cover the ripped seats. At least that was a job we could do when we had the gear to do it with. I started a list.

When the place was clean enough to use for eating, we started on cleaning the kitchen and fridges. The oven and cooking gear was just like in my old kitchen, only bigger. There was a huge dishwasher and a griddle for frying things. I figured that I could have the place ready to go in a week but Lou had other ideas.

"You can open in the morning," she said confidently. "Grand openings can wait. We can have a crowd here for 8 a.m. station time."

I hedged; it was all a bit hasty. "What about advertising, stock and help?"

"There are things in the freezer. Munro will get your delivery. I'm surprised that he said that, it's not like him to help, but he'll do it if he said he would."

"Maybe he's got a plan?" said Terri.

I could think of a good one, just give me the stock and let me go; let me make a balls of it. I could manage that on my own. He could stand back and watch.

"You'll have eggs and bacon and milk," she added. "No-one will be too judgemental on your first day, as long as the coffee is hot and there's something to eat."

I liked her, I liked both of them, and Tina too. If everyone else was this friendly and helpful, perhaps things would be OK.

"Will you be here in the morning?" I had my fingers crossed and toes plaited.

"We can't," said Terri. "We both have measurements to do early in the morning for the next couple of days. You've got Cy." Obviously they had never seen him at 8 a.m. Actually I don't think anyone had, unless he had been up all night.

"Call me at seven," he suggested. "I'll be here." He sounded willing but then he always did; at nine in the morning when he appeared looking innocent, I could remind him, and he would flutter his lashes and apologise profusely.

"Don't worry too much," said Lou. "They won't mind queueing a bit, they'll just be happy to be away from Munro's profit margin. Tell you what," she mused, "we'll have a word, see if we can find anyone to help you out."

"Mike had enough helpers," suggested Terri. "At least that's what he called them. I'm sure that we can get one of the more respectable ones to muck in if we ask them nicely."

"Thanks." I meant it too. If I was going to open, there were a few other jobs to do, quite a few of the café's lightbulbs were out, and the ones that remained were red, fine for a bar or a club but not really ideal for a café. I'd spotted a box of spares in the stores.

"Get a ladder," I told Cy, "and we can sort out the illuminations."

Lou stopped me. "You need an electrician for that," she said. "Safety rules, it's a fire hazard."

"How much will that cost me?" I needed to know, I had money but not a lot of it.

"It won't cost you anything," Terri said. "It's fabric and safety work so it's all part of the rental deal, just call up Wallis and complain, or go to the admin office, someone will come along and do it." Good to know, as long as it wasn't Wallis himself doing it.

I put it on my list.

We chatted while we worked and I learned a lot. There were over eight hundred people on the station; there was a farm for basic produce, and there weren't many eligible men. A lot of the workers' partners lived here, as well as us and the diner there were a few basic shops. Most people had jobs, if not mining then on the farm or the support and administration services. There was an infirmary and a police force, called the guards. Everything a city would have.

Lou confirmed that all the garbage had to be inspected before disposal, hence the human Popsicle in my freezer. And there weren't many eligible men. I got that twice so it must have been important.

I found the rulebook too; it was a doorstop of a thing, good for insomnia; or treating ganglions. And a small book about the station, produced by the mining company that owned the place. It said that it was a resident's guide but it wasn't really much more than an advert for the company, full of boasting but there was a section on the technical details of the station.

That looked very interesting, it may have been propaganda but it was still quite an achievement to have built the thing in the first place. And it told me why it was here, on page one. There was a lot of profit in the things that they were mining, things that we had run out of on Earth. There was also a list of the most important regulations for safety. I would have to give that a good read.

Cy didn't involve himself with cleaning; he was too concerned with his nails and his soft hands. At least he didn't sit around; you couldn't tell him what to do, he would pick a job for himself. Once he had decided what he fancied doing he would go and get on with it and was a tireless worker. He decided his talents would be best employed making an inventory of all the supplies we had, the use by dates and all the things we needed.

"You'll never reach half of it," he said and of course he was right. While he was in the store doing that, the twins and I worked and chatted. After a couple of hours, there was a noise outside as a motorised vehicle of some sort pulled up.

"Delivery for Miss Pett," a deep male voice shouted, I ran to the door, nearly getting trampled in the rush.

This must be the run-around that Munro was on about; I had seen several of the electric vehicles on the way up from the shuttle. I'd nearly been run over by one. This one was a weird sort of cross between a supermarket trolley and a small van; two seats at the front and a large basket arrangement at the back.

There may not have been many eligible men on the station but this was definitely one of them, and he was from the school of good-lookingness. Automatically I checked his fingers – clean, there were no rings, but he was bound to be in demand.

The basket was piled with packs of dairy produce and I saw some eggs and sausages in there as well as fresh vegetables. Hopefully there was some bacon; Cy was partial to a bacon sandwich and I might need to bribe him to get out of bed.

"It's from the farm," he said. "Sign here," Munro had been as good as his word, and quick; which was suspicious.

"Hi," I fluttered. "I'm Andi." God; it sounded like I was desperate.

"Hello, Andi," he replied. "I'm Heynrik, with a 'Y'."

Why not? I thought, just as Lou, or Terri, or both, shouted from behind me, "Hi, Heynrik," they said.

I saw him first, then I realised that I hadn't as he answered, "Oh hello, Lou. Are you working here again? That's good to know, I'll see you when I deliver."

"I'm Terri," she replied.

"No you're not," he answered, as quick as a flash. "I can see the mole."

Hmm, there was history here; maybe a little Q and A was in order. I had the twins onside, no need to let a bloke spoil things by coming between us. I was sure we could come to some sort of arrangement that left me clear to pursue him.

Heynrik fiddled around with the basket thing and it detached from the cab. He wheeled it into the café and helped unload it, stacking the shelves and fridges with the produce. All the mouldy stuff was in a small pile where we had thrown it while we cleaned out the shelves. Lou made him put as much of the stock as she could on the high and low shelves, I swear that she did it deliberately; just to help him show off his muscles, because all the time he was stretching and bending she was watching appreciatively. After he had done that he loaded all the mouldy food into the basket.

"This'll go to the incinerator," he told me. "If you can have it all bagged up ready next time it'll be quicker. There's no charge for this load, next time you'll have it automatically taken off your account. Do you want the same arrangement as Mike had, a delivery every two days?"

"Yes," said Lou. "Until she gets an idea of how much to order, just keep it simple, whatever Mike had on order, bring it."

"OK," he said. "You can always pass an extra order—"

"Through the admin office," we all said at once, and then we laughed.

We didn't get much more done after he left, it seemed like a good time to take a break for tea. I wanted to ask Lou about Heynrik's availability for more than delivering foodstuffs but while we were drinking it Lou looked at her watch and announced that they would have to go and do some work for the government; only reasonable I suppose as it was them who were paying their wages.

"We have some stars and things to measure," she said, in a voice that indicated that whatever it was, it was way above my capacity to understand. "And the orbital angle will soon be right."

Terri giggled. "And don't you dare," she warned, "tell us that it's still daytime will you."

I didn't but then I hadn't really thought about it. I guess that it was always night outside, in space there was no real day; it was all kept the same as on Earth for convenience. My interrogation would have to wait.

"The whole station is just as busy round the clock," Lou said.

"You might not know it but the diner is open twenty-four seven; you do realise that after you get started, you'll have to do the same to keep up. There's people coming on and off shift all the time, everyone on the station works on the basis that it's day and night when you decide that it is. Partners tend to keep to the same routines, it makes for healthier relationships."

If the place was running all hours, that would explain Mike's 'helpers'. Great! I would be serving all three meals at the same time. How was I going to keep awake all the time and when was I going to make some bloody cupcakes?

"We'll drop you some boiler suits when we finish tonight," they shouted as they walked away.

"What's the plan then, Andi?" Cy asked me as the shutters rolled down, it was getting late. I had made a start on preparing food and I had tried to put in a call about the lights. Considering that I was expected to work all hours, the electricians were off till the morning unless it was an emergency. And changing my bulbs didn't qualify. A search of the stores had found more bedding, towels and other essentials, including boiler suits for Cy and me.

Lou had popped back with some boiler suits, I took them and thanked her, even though we had found some, it was a kind thing to do and I wanted to keep her onside. I could explain later. She also said that she had spoken to someone called Maz; she would be here to help us open up at eight. She couldn't stop; she had to get back to do a little more light stargazing or whatever.

"I've got a list, Cy," I waved it at him. "But right now, I've had enough for one day." It wasn't a long list, and I had done some of it.

Sort out what I needed for the morning; done.

Make some stock; urgh – 4 a.m. start.

Get the lights fixed; pending.

Order stuff to repair the seats; pending.

Get some advertising sorted and snoop about; to be arranged.

Apart from that, we were ready for business.

"If we can get through tomorrow," I said, "then we can sort out a proper opening day and lay on the dancing girls."

He raised an eyebrow. "Seriously, dancing girls? Not very inclusive, is it?"

"I'm working on it," I told him. "Watch this space."

"And what about the body in the freezer?" He sounded bothered. "Are we just going to forget it? Seriously, Andi, we should go, before we get sucked in any deeper."

I'd thought about it and could see that Tina and the twins were right, if Munro knew about the bank, he would know if I tried to leave. If he had clout he wouldn't be afraid to use it. And it might be convenient for him to pin Mr Icicle's death on me somehow, however improbable it sounded. I didn't know how things worked here and wasn't willing to take the chance. Besides, I wanted to make a go of the café.

"No, we're here and we're staying. If we run, where are we going to go?"

He looked dubious. "I think it's a bad idea, how are we ever going to find out who killed this bloke? Nobody knows us well enough to admit it and why do we even care? If some gangster wants to run this dump, let him!"

"Look, Cy," I said. "I'll have a good nose around after the rush tomorrow when you're running things. I'll be the new arrival, it's a good excuse to poke my nose into all sorts of corners."

"I don't like it. Someone's already killed one man, who's to say you're not next?"

"If I'm that visible, I'll be safe," I said with a lot less confidence than I felt.

"That'll be what our guest thought." He jerked his head in the general direction of the freezer. "Just be careful."

That was a sobering thought. "See you at seven."

Chapter 7

My alarm bleeped, it couldn't be 4 a.m. already. Before I had slept, I had made up the bed properly; on my way to the spare room I had spotted two mattresses on Cy's bed, who did he think he was? He must have grabbed the one I had my eye on while I was getting him some towels; ungrateful or what! Well, he was going to have to make do with one like everyone else, I thought, as I dragged my prize down the corridor. He would find out when he eventually came out of the bathroom. Hopefully he wouldn't cause a one man water shortage with all his preening. Where did the water come from anyhow?

I reckoned that I had come up with a plan, or at least a scheme. Using my naiveté as a cover I could explore the station whilst trying to promote the café, meet people and look around, find out more about Mike and who might want him dead.

Sort of dumb blonde mode; only with black hair. It seemed a bit harsh on Lou and Terri as I thought it, oh well, pardon my stereotype. They played on it, why not me. I had wanted to have a look at the guidebook but I was too tired.

I looked at my watch, hoping that I had set the alarm wrong. Nope, it was 4 a.m. alright. I got up and in a reflex action I turned on my hair straighteners. They would heat up while I had a quick wash, ready to tame what my mother used to call the 'bird's-nest'. In fact they would heat up almost instantly, as I knew to my cost.

After untangling my hair and getting my face sorted, I put on one of the boiler suits. There, I was ready for work. The boiler suit was marked 'small' and that made me feel better, my mother used to say shortish and roundish. I idly wondered if the twins' suits were marked 'tall, thin, blonde'.

Strangely, it felt good to be dressed in overalls, not my usual attire but in the same way that a school uniform made everyone equal, I could see the attraction. It made me feel that I was somehow a part of the station, part of the scenery. And it meant that I didn't have to agonise over what to wear for ages, it was either the boiler suit or… the other boiler suit. A pair of pumps and I was done.

I needed to get the café running so that I could leave Cy in charge while I snooped about. Easier said than done, at eight in the morning Cy wasn't at his best, if the customers were rattling at the shutter he would be at their heels like a disagreeable terrier. And although there was this Maz coming to help, she would have to be Saint Maz the Eternally Placid to cope with pre-lunch Cy.

By four-thirty I was up to my elbows in cake mix, they would need something to sell. I could have got cakes pre-made but I wanted to start as I meant to go on. Everywhere needed a hook and home baked was going to be mine. I could remember recipes from the things I used to help my mother make, back on Earth. And I wasn't really as bad at cooking as everyone made out, on a good day my efforts were mostly edible.

Lou and Terri had said that they would bake for me and their offerings yesterday were better than my best work but that was in the future; right now I reckoned that I needed croissants, muffins, cupcakes, a sponge and a cheesecake. And this needed to be a good day, so I had to concentrate. If there were people thinking it was morning, afternoon and night all at the same time, my bases needed covering. There were lunchy things in the freezer and potatoes that could be baked.

As for breakfasts, thanks to Munro we had sausages, bacon and eggs; that would do for a start. And I thought I had seen some mushrooms in the fridge. We could always do some fries as well. I would need to print menus. I had seen a chalkboard behind the bar; that would have to do for a start.

I wondered about advertising, the twins had said I wouldn't need to but a few posters might help. There was a tannoy system that blasted all sorts of safety messages and other bits of information all around the public spaces; I had heard it when we arrived. Perhaps I could get them to announce the grand opening. Tina could also tell all her mates. If Lou and Terri were right and everyone knew everything anyway, I might not need to push too hard.

Oh hell, there was just so much to think of. I broke eggs into the mixer bowl and spent ten minutes getting broken bits of shell out of the mix; concentrate, Andi! I told myself.

The kitchen was well set up and had all the equipment to make life easy. And I admit that I cheated with the croissants, using pre-made dough from the load that Heynrik had brought over. By seven, I had everything made and the last batch was in the oven. Cakes were cooling, the dishwasher was stacked and running. The smell of fresh baking filled the air as I went back towards the spare room. To my surprise, I had actually enjoyed the work. Along with the boiler suit, the act of making something for the benefit of the station made me feel part of it. And the stuff that was coming out of the oven so far wasn't burnt or raw so that was a bonus. I had noticed that I was actually singing to myself as I made icing.

I hammered on the door. "Seven, time to get up Cy," I shouted.

"I'll be along," he mumbled, believing him, I went to put the boiler and the coffee machine on; as I went into the café and fiddled about I swear I heard the murmur of conversation outside. Panic started to set in, probably first day nerves. I went back and called Cy again. "Alright, I'm coming," he said. It was nearly seven fifteen, almost time to get the grill and the griddle on for bacon and sausages. This was ridiculous, why couldn't we have breakfast separate from coffee time?

There was a ping from the kitchen as I realised that along with my fear, I could smell the tang of soon to be overdone pastry products. Running back into the kitchen I opened the oven doors and grabbed a towel. To my relief, I was just in time. The croissants were a very dark golden. Where was Cy?

I iced the cooled cakes and put the warm croissants in the display cabinet, then I called Cy again, got another, "OK, OK," and started cooking sausages.

It was almost time; maybe this Maz would be helpful, if she had been persuaded. I could definitely hear noise from outside now, it sounded like a swarm of bees, and then suddenly it stopped. There was a woman's voice, then silence.

I went back and called Cy once more. "It's quarter to eight, get up and help me," I pleaded. There was no reply but I saw that the bathroom door was shut, I could hear the shower running, he must have got up after the last call; less than forty-five minutes was some sort of new record.

I went to the front door and pressed the button. The shutter rolled up; there must have been about thirty people outside. They all looked at me as I opened the door, it felt uncomfortable, like judging time at some sort of show. The lights were still flickering and the alleyway was in semi-darkness, which was another job for the electrician when I could get hold of one.

There were miners in greasy overalls, a couple of suited men and a selection of women. The disco effect from the lights made their movements seem jerky, like a crowd of zombies ready to attack.

At the front of the throng was a sweet-faced old lady, in the same boiler suit as me and a lot of the crowd, although I could see that quite a few of the women had added flashes of colour and other adornments to the basic garment. She smiled at me.

"Good morning, dear," she said. She turned back to the crowd. "Now then, let's have an orderly queue," she said. "Working people first. And give poor Ms Pett a chance on her first day." Everyone shuffled and did what they were told – impressive.

She stepped inside and closed the door on them. "I'm Maz," she said. "Lou asked me to help you out; I used to run the place for Mike while he had a... break." I got the impression that she really meant something else but didn't know me well enough to say. "You might think that I'm bossy but I'm afraid I can't help it, I used to be a teacher and I learnt it was the best way, you should never give children any sign of weakness." She had a twinkle in her eye as she said it. "That Mike was a cheeky so-and-so," she went on. "I didn't take any nonsense from him but oh, I could tell you some things."

I hoped she could as well. I liked her immediately; she was like my gran, effortlessly in charge, confident in her abilities and very shrewd. I would just have to make sure she never went to the freezer. But then her approach reminded me of school and I reverted to the younger me. She was a teacher; I went into 'rabbit in the lights' mode, you could blame the convent for that.

"Now have you worked in a café before, dear?" she asked. It was no good, it had happened again. I couldn't answer her. All I could do was shake my head. If she thought it was a strange time to start she didn't say so. "What do you want me to do then?"

Everything, I thought but I still didn't answer. I had this thing about female teachers, they made me feel inadequate and reduced me to a silent, sweating wreck, it was a long story.

She tried again. "What don't you want to do then?" I was frozen; now that the moment had arrived I couldn't think of a thing to say. Lots of people would have been shocked at my silence. Maz just took it all in her stride. She must have recognised her natural prey.

She smiled in understanding. "Tell you what, how about you let me do the bulk of it," she said. "Just pass me things when I ask you for them. The cakes smell lovely by the way. Now where's the bacon, there were some miners in the queue and they'll want bacon rolls."

Oh God! I had made all the cakes but had completely forgotten all about any sort of bread. She saw my face drop and did the teacher thing where they read your mind.

"No bread eh? Don't worry, dear. I know Mike used to keep some in the freezer," she said. "I'll go and grab it; we can defrost it in the microwave and crisp the crusts under the grill."

Chapter 8

She must have decided that I was a total fool, I hadn't made it hard for her, but she was just too kind to say it. She turned and was on the way to the store as my brain caught up and I realised what was happening.

"Nooo!" it was meant to be a simple word but it came out like a strangled plea. "The freezer's locked." I said it as one word and I could feel my neck go red, just like it used to do at school. I couldn't let her into the freezer.

She gave me a funny look and you could almost see the wheels turning. "It's OK, dear; I know where Mike keeps the key."

I had given her a clue; there was something funny about the freezer, and she was a teacher, they could be tricky. I would have to think of another reason why she had to stay out of it. If I wasn't careful, the more I protested the more interesting it would become. And I had to leave her here while I snooped. I wasn't even open and I'd already managed to dig myself into a huge hole.

"I'll get it, I need to call Cy again anyway. You carry on here."

"OK," she shrugged.

As I made my way towards the door, the man himself made an entrance, he must have been listening and he had two plastic bags in his hands. One contained frozen rolls, the other loaves. He had taken the trouble to find a striped apron and looked almost like a chef.

"Are these what you wanted?" he asked innocently. "I heard you as I was coming out and grabbed them on the way past."

Her eyes narrowed, she knew that the bedrooms were the other side of the store; he couldn't have been 'coming past'.

"We are going to need to have a little chat, dear," she said. I felt a detention coming on. She turned to Cy. "Thank you. Cy, isn't it? I've heard about you. I'm Maz. Now don't just stand there, no doubt you're late as it is. Get the bread into the big microwave; take it out of the bags first or it'll sweat. Defrost for ten minutes I should think, then into a warm oven to brown. And get ready to start frying eggs and bacon."

I wouldn't have spoken to Cy like that, and I'd known him for years. I'd tried it once, a long time ago. In return he had explained several things I might like to consider doing, which were either impossible, illegal or sounded dangerous. But she was in full teacher mode. His school days must have been like mine because I actually saw him shudder.

"Right away, Maz," he meekly said and turned away. Wow!

"He seems like a nice man," she said. "Are you… a couple?"

She might have been sharp but she had missed that one. I'd leave him to explain, it would be something they could talk about while I was gone.

"Business partners," I replied. In a way I was pleased; there was a chink in her armour, she wasn't Sister Grace, the infallible overlord of my convent school, finding perpetual fault and making me feel like I was a waste of everyone's time. And I had learned to cope with her, in the end I even got to like her.

I shouldn't forget that Maz wasn't my teacher; she was a lady who was kind. Kind enough to be bothered to get up early and come down here to help us.

"You take the orders, dear," she said, "and I'll do the drinks. Cy can cook anything we need and you can deliver to the tables. It'll give you a chance to say hello to everyone."

We opened up and they poured in, forming an orderly queue. I took the orders, writing everything down on a pad that I had spotted by the payment terminal. Payment! What was I going to charge for coffee? I've been selling for years and in the world I used to inhabit there were no price lists, if you wanted one of my creations you paid what I asked, if you needed to know the price before I started you were in the wrong place.

This was different. "What do we charge for coffee and things?" I asked Maz as she worked.

I got another teacher look. "Don't worry, dear," she said patiently. "It's simple, we charge just a little less than the diner." She produced a laminated sheet, it was the diner's menu, she must have grabbed it on the way past this morning. "As long as we're cheaper than them, and we can be because they were exploiting their monopoly, then we'll be OK."

Had she been up all night working these things out? Or was she just picking up where Mike's departure had stopped her. Why hadn't I looked at the menu before I'd started making things? Either way, I said a silent 'thank you' to Lou and Terri. And to Tina.

We settled into a routine, everyone was friendly and the queue never seemed to get any smaller. I met some of the miners, big tough looking men who carried their boots in one hand and apologised for the dirty overalls. They all had names like Rik or Grant and seemed puzzled to find that Andi wasn't a bloke. They took their drinks and automatically went into the far corner, where they chatted while they waited for their food. They seemed as scared of Maz as I was.

The men in suits must have been on their way somewhere, they asked for takeaway coffee and croissants, paid and left. That was another thing, Munro was right about the money, they all paid with contactless cards; I never saw any cash. I needed one of those cards, as long as there were no shoe shops.

The women hopped onto the barstools or sat around the tables. There were a lot of what you'd call yummy mummies, except that there were no children, in fact there was no-one who looked under about eighteen. That was strange!

Clearly there were enough folk on the station fed-up with Munro's joint to want to come in here. Unless they were just curious about the new owner. Whatever; they were here and if they liked the place they would be back.

I got so many people saying, "Hello, I'm whoever; Lou, or Terri or Tina told me you were opening" that it was impossible for my brain to catalogue all of them. They all knew Maz though; she introduced me to all the customers and in true teacher fashion knew everyone by name. A lot of them asked if I needed any help, waitressing, cooking or cleaning; I started to make a list of their names and phone numbers. I would be able to quiz them about Mike; it might give me some clues. A few looked wistfully around to see if there was any sign of him after all, as if they wanted to see him again. Maybe I could make some extra money charging for visits to the freezer?

Cy was behaving himself; he was coping with the stream of orders. Bacon rolls and breakfasts started appearing through the serving hatch and I left the queue for a moment to carry them over to the miners. They thanked me and attacked their food. As I was serving them I could see tiredness etched in their faces; it must be some job out there.

I thought that we would be run off our feet but Maz was a natural, if anything I was getting in her way. She coped with orders, serving, making coffee and taking payments almost without seeming to move.

I thought that it all seemed chaotic for a while but I surprised myself by getting into the swing of things. After an hour or so I actually began to enjoy the process of dispensing drinks and breakfasts. Cy had kept up the supply of hot food from the kitchen, some people even bought my cakes and in the end the rush dwindled.

"Tell me, Maz," I asked in a lull between customers, the place was nearly full and conversation hummed in the background, "how come there are no children here; are they all at school or something?"

She gave me a look; again I thought she was despairing at my lack of knowledge. "Station rules, dear," she explained. "No children allowed, and under eighteens only if they have a job."

"Oh." It seemed a little harsh. "I thought that when you said you were a teacher, that there would be a school or something here." She shook her head.

"The management think it's too dangerous for children," she said. "They could do something daft and blow the place up. It's very strict; if you get pregnant here you're on the next shuttle out. I was a teacher on Mars, I came here when I retired, I was on my own by then and I thought it would be nice and quiet."

That seemed a shame, not that I was desperate to have kids running around, but it did give the place more character, maybe people just worked here to earn a good wage before settling down somewhere else. And it was a shame that Maz was on her own. I didn't like to ask her the reason.

"And is it?"

She shook her head. "I preferred Mars, less people, lots of open space, high ceilings; you could almost forget that you were enclosed sometimes. There was always a place you could go for a bit of peace. It's like an overcrowded goldfish bowl in here."

Just then, Lou, or was it Terri, got to the front of the queue.

"Hi, Maz. Morning, Andi," she chirped. "It's nice and busy in here. Our messages must have got around. Do you fancy a quick tour, Andi? I'm off work for a few hours. Love the overalls. I thought that size would be about right for you."

"Hi," I said, checking out the mole situation, definitely Terri. "I'd love to, if Maz can manage." It sounded like it could be fun, and the chance to do some snooping. As long as Cy was happy.

"Oy!" shouted the man himself, leaning through the hatch from the kitchen. "What about saying hello to me then, Terri? I'm slaving away in here all alone and nobody notices." How could he tell which one it was from that distance?

Terri walked round the counter, leant through the hatch and pecked him on the cheek. "Hello yourself," she purred. "Loving the chef's outfit." How did he do it, have them eating out of his hand like that? Maybe they just felt safe around him.

"Go," said Maz. "I can manage as long as Cy carries on cooking."

"Course I will," he shouted through the hatch. "I'm enjoying myself, clear off!" he actually sounded sincere, not his usual sarcastic reply. Maybe he really was enjoying himself.

Chapter 9

"We'll start at the top, that's where we work," she said, as we walked down the alleyway towards the lifts. "Did you get a chance to look at the company guide?"

I had to admit that I hadn't as we walked into the better lit part of the station. There were people everywhere and quite a few of the run-arounds bobbing in and out on their rubber tyres, giving little warning of their approach. They all looked basically the same, a two-seat cab at the front but they were fitted with various different backs. The sort of thing you see in airports. Their tyres squeaked on the metal of the decks as they turned and dodged through the human traffic. I found the silent motion alarming, although the drivers seemed to accept the constant stopping as part of the deal.

"Look out!" said Terri, grabbing me and pulling me away from one that had designs on my knees. "Keep out of the yellow check pattern on the deck, they usually stay inside it." I hadn't noticed the markings. "It's just after shift change, really busy, it'll quieten down shortly."

We passed the diner; I couldn't help but notice that it was practically empty. The barista was polishing his equipment listlessly; he gave us a filthy look as we passed. We went past the main lifts, into a small alley like the approach to the café, only this one was better lit. There was a small lift tucked away in a corner and Terri used a plastic card to open the door.

"This is the secure lift; you need a card to open it. It's the only way to get to some of the working areas. Stay close to me." She pressed a button and we rose quickly, my knees sagged and my ears popped. The numbers rolled back to zero. "This is the observatory. There's a lot of expensive gear up here; please don't touch anything."

The trouble was, I knew from past experience that the harder that I tried to keep away the more I would somehow be dragged closer. It was like a magnet of embarrassing clumsiness. Telling me not to touch something was like asking me to break it in the most improbable and non-repairable way that I could.

We arrived and stepped out; there was a flight of steps leading up. It got darker as we climbed in a spiral and I stumbled in the dark, grabbing the handrail for support.

"Why is it getting darker," I asked. "It helps your vision adjust," Terri whispered. As I reached the top and looked around, I almost forgot to breathe.

The ceiling of the observatory was transparent. Everything above desk height was see-through. There were banks of computers on low desks but otherwise the view was uninterrupted. And what a view! I felt like I was perched at the centre of the universe. Were there really that many stars? Saturn was over to one side and our sun, no more than a bright tennis ball, was away in the other direction. I could see the planet, the rings and several moons, all floating in front of a backdrop of scattered diamonds.

I stepped over to the glass or whatever it was. Looking down, the bulk of the station lay below me, dark and featureless. It was so much bigger than I had thought, stretching away in all directions, its disc hiding the stars. We were slightly offset from the middle and you couldn't see over the edge of it. "It's all painted to absorb light," Terri explained. "And our telescope is over there." She pointed to a shape on the edge of the station, articulated like a crane. "We can swing it around from here," she explained, "and for the bits that the station masks, we have another on the bottom, on the opposite side."

Lou was working on a large flat table, lit from inside, she had what looked like X-ray plates laid out and was peering at them through a large, brass framed magnifying glass on a stalk.

"Hi, Andi," she said, standing up and rubbing her back. "Bloody table's built for short people... Oops, sorry."

Behind me Terri giggled and then stopped abruptly. We couldn't all be tall and graceful like them. I was used to it. I pretended not to notice; anyway, there was no malice in her voice.

"Why do you look at the pictures with a magnifying glass," I asked, "when you have all these computers to analyse things?" I stood as far as I could from everything, trying to keep my hands by my sides, fighting the urge to touch something, anything!

"They're not as sensitive as an eye," she said. "And there are so many things to programme in to make sure they do it properly. We don't miss as much as they do, and we do it quicker."

"They analyse the bits we spot," added Terri. "Once we tell them where to look." The two of them bent over a picture and started talking in a foreign language, all red-shifts and quasars or something.

As my vision adjusted I could make out quite a few other people in the room, working at computers or just looking out at the view. But I suspect they would say they were studying things. There was an air of studious calm that I couldn't quite adjust to, hence my present occupation, important though it was. I'd never been academic, I was never able to shut up and concentrate for long enough to work out what the teacher was going on about. But here, I felt like I understood completely, I was a part of all that I could see. I almost wanted to step outside and just... belong. Fortunately there wasn't a door; I'd have been opening it.

Seeing Lou and Terri work made me realise just what an act the whole twins thing was, here they were in their element, single minded and professional. They ignored me and carried on with their technical discussion, that was OK though, I could have stood here forever.

"Andi, sorry, we got lost there," said Terri, after what might have been a few moments or may been a lot longer. I had no idea and wasn't bothered. You could see just how contrived time was here. "Let's go down to the farm, there's a lot more to see."

"Can I come back up here again?" I asked in a whisper, like you did in church, somehow it didn't seem appropriate to talk loudly. "I've never seen anything like it."

"We don't notice," said Lou. "It's all familiar, you can come up with one of us, just ask. But you'll soon get bored with it." I didn't agree, after London and the enclosed spaces I'd been in, this was freedom. This was what I had run to find, I knew it then. The memory of Tina offering us a trip in a mining craft even interested me.

We got back into the lift and went down two floors. We got out of the lift and walked back down an alley to an open space similar to the one on our own deck.

"Every deck has the same basic layout," Terri explained. "We're back at the main lifts."

Opposite the lift was an airlock. I knew that because there were big signs that said 'Warning, Airlock!'.

"Where are we going now?" I asked as she typed in a code. The door opened and we walked in. Didn't we need spacesuits or something if we were going out of an airlock? Maybe they were inside. The outer doors closed behind us with a clang. The space was empty, just a metal box. I was about to ask what was going on when there was a hiss and a flash of red light. I felt my face and body being sprayed with a sweet smelling chemical, like hairspray. I jumped, it was cold, and then it evaporated in a blast of warm air.

"Don't worry," Terri reassured me. "It's just disinfectant, you'll see."

"We're not going outside are we?" I tried not to sound worried.

"Of course not," she said as the door opened and I stepped into a sight I never thought I'd see again.

Chapter 10

If I had been surprised at the sight of the cosmos, this was just surreal. The doors had opened on a waving field of wheat, bathed in artificial sunlight. It was scattered with wild flowers in every shade. In the distance I was sure I could see cows grazing, under trees for goodness' sake. I just stood, unable to speak. Bees buzzed. I shut my mouth before one flew in. There was nothing like this on Earth any more, anywhere.

"This is the second farm level," Terri said. "There're two more levels below this one, there's one above us as well but it's fallow at the moment, so there's nothing to see except bare soil. And there's a park underneath that, between the farm and the apartments, a public space where we can relax, play games and picnic. We grow most of our own food on the station, basics admittedly but it's enough for everyone to live on. It's only the luxuries that come up on the shuttle. And they're working on them."

We walked down a path between the crops. Looking closer, I could see that the soil was held in large depressions in the metal of the deck, we walked on bare steel.

"How is this even possible?" There were so many questions, I gave up trying to frame them, just walked and gazed. Terri launched into an explanation; thankfully it was in words I could understand, given my sensory overload.

"They call the fields pans," she said. "Each pan has a different crop and they're rotated to keep the soil fertile. There's plumbing in the deck and sprinklers overhead for watering. You should read the guidebook, the bit about how the farm got started, it's fascinating!"

I was amazed by the sight; it was difficult for my mind to take it all in. There was a rustling noise in the wheat or whatever it was to my right, suddenly a rabbit jumped out and ran in front of me. It bounced twice on the metal and disappeared into the green stems of unripe corn on the other side.

That was the icing on the cake for me. I love rabbits, it reminded me of Horlicks, my pet when I was little. A homely touch out here, a billion miles from Queens Park in more ways than one.

There was a man doing something in amongst the wheat, he must have heard us because he stood and waved. He wandered over, he was tall and broad-shouldered and my mind went into overdrive. I stopped slouching and stood upright, sucking my stomach in, just in case he was single. When he got closer, I could see that he was about fifteen years older than me, fit looking with a kind face. Handsome and dignified. Just what I thought was my type. It was just a pity that they never thought that I was their type.

"Hi, Terri," he said. "I was up here when I heard the airlock; this must be the mysterious Andi."

Hang on, was I mysterious? I'd never been that, my mother used to say I was too obvious. And how did everyone else but me tell the twins apart instantly? And wasn't this all a bit coincidental? Maybe Terri had set this up before she invited me on a tour.

"Hi, Derek," she said. "Yep, this is Andi. Derek is in charge of the farm, he's a genius and he keeps us all fed. I thought you might like to see where the stuff that Heynrik delivers comes from."

"Hello, Andi," he said, blushing slightly, now he was right up next to me I could see sadness in his eyes and the weight of responsibility on his shoulders. But there was something about him alright. "Excuse me not shaking hands." He waved them around; I could see that they were smeared with something; I didn't want to know what. That was a shame, I had been anticipating contact. "I know all about you, Davina told me last night." I tried not to look disappointed; he had someone.

Derek laughed. "The one thing that's constant here, everyone knows everything; there are no secrets; right, Terri?"

Now it was Terri's turn to blush. "I do hope there are still a few," she replied primly.

"Andi," she said, "Davina is Derek's daughter; she's one of the farm administrators. She heard about you from Mr Wallis's daughter, Elise." Ah; that meant that at some time Mr G must have been attractive to someone; perhaps I had been doing him a disservice? Or perhaps he had changed. I was contemplating that and Derek's situation but he was still talking.

"Terri, Davina has left her job," he said. "She wanted to look after me, I told her she shouldn't but she insisted; she's just like her mother was. Can you try and talk some sense into her?"

Terri assured him that she would. I was trying to keep up with his domestic arrangements.

"What do you think about our little operation?" he asked me; well what could I say? This was just the latest in the series of jaw-dropping moments in my immediate past. Catching Trevor bouncing on Masie had started it, then me actually getting on a spaceship, then deciding to open the café and now this, a farm in space. I'd heard of the farms orbiting around Earth, everyone knew about them, here it was unexpected; I thought that this was just a mining station.

But it made sense. It would take a fleet of ships to supply the food for all these people, better to grow most of it here. Farms on Earth weren't like this any more; the space was too precious to waste. Everything was crammed in and so fertilised to make it provide a bigger yield that the taste had been knocked out of it by the time you saw it in a shop. Even in the short time that I'd been here I had noticed the real taste, not the artificial taste, of all the food. It was one great thing about the place.

I'd considered stopping on one of the orbiting farms when we had left Earth, but they were too close to Trevor for my liking. We had kept going, and now I had ended up on one anyway.

"It's amazing, how do you get all the power for the lights?" I hadn't thought about how the place was functioning at all, or even the size of it, it just was. And that was the first question that came into my mind. I felt pleased, I'd managed to ask something intelligent; Derek wouldn't think I was stupid.

"That's a good question," he said with a smile. "We usually get something daft; people are so surprised they ask if the cows have names, or if the roots go through the walls."

I just tried to look intelligent; hopefully I wouldn't have to keep it up for too long.

"All the station's power comes from an electro-chemical plant in the core," he said. "Think of it like a big battery. It's safer than a fusion reactor and there are plenty of raw materials—" he waved his hand, "—out there in the big black. As a by-product the waste heat and the methane helps to keep us all warm. The plants produce oxygen and everyone, humans and animals, give us fertilizer."

So that explained why we weren't all glowing. I was pleased to hear that we wouldn't be radiated or whatever it was called. It was one less way to go, even though it still left quite a few others. And the fertiliser bit, I guess it was natural but it was enough information.

"You said cows, are they cows over there?" I had to know, Derek smiled again, he was smiling at me a lot, if he had Davina, there must be a Mrs Derek though.

"Yes, and we have pigs and sheep, chickens too. We've managed to develop a complete eco-system, like on Earth. It wasn't working properly at one point and we worked out that we needed rabbits to balance things up. Don't ask me why, I'm a farmer not a planetary engineer but with them, yields are up and everything works."

His voice was filled with pride; I suspected that he never really got the praise he deserved from the rest of the inhabitants, only complaints if there were ever a shortage of eggs.

"I think what you've done here is amazing. Have you got any fish?"

He looked pleased with himself. "Well, now that you come to mention it, we're putting in some tanks on the lower deck, that's where we have all our offices and processing equipment. But we have a lot of problems to overcome, fresh water's OK and we even have a trout stream but we want salt water so we can do lobsters and stuff, we need to replicate ocean movement somehow."

"How about putting the tanks on springs and shaking them around?" I blurted out. I don't know where that idea came from; I just wanted to keep talking to him, hear the deep voice and see the sad brown eyes. I wanted to find out why they were sad and make them happy. Oh crap, I thought, I've gone and said a dozy thing.

He shook his head. "Do you know, that's not a bad idea. I'll have to think about it but you might be onto something. There are so many things to get right; it's hard to keep up with it all. It's like Earth really, just on a smaller scale."

If he was building another Earth out here, who or what did that make him? I gazed across the Eden that this man had produced and wanted to share it.

And he was more right than he realised, even though I had only been here a short while, I could already see that the station was a lot like Earth in other ways; there was an official boss, a real boss behind the scenes and lots of things that some people didn't want others to know.

Chapter 11

Derek excused himself. "I have to go; it was lovely to meet you, Andi. Make sure that you come back and see me again, and if you want to know anything, just come up and ask." He moved away between the waving stems. I planned on it; I was sad to see him go.

"He's a lovely man," Terri said. I wondered if she had noticed my interest, obviously she had when she continued, "But so awful for him, his wife just upped and jumped on a shuttle while he was at work, she left him a note, said that she had had enough of the station and that she was going back to Mars. Davina stayed here to look after him. We all keep an eye out for him; he gets so distracted he forgets to eat sometimes. Davina leaving her job is bad news; I'll have to talk to her, see what's going on."

She didn't elaborate. It seemed like this Davina was only looking out for her father; he was obviously a good catch. At least it meant that he was available.

"The next deck is like this, then there's the processing plant for the produce, do you want to watch cows being milked and stuff like that?"

I could miss that out, it would make a good reason to come back and see Derek again. And my mind was overloaded with everything that I had seen.

"It's where the greenhouses are," she said. "They grow tomatoes, strawberries and melons, amongst other things." It sounded more interesting than cows but I still wasn't gripped. I had my plan. I could pass on that one too.

"That's fine by me."

"And the park and the accommodation decks, we'll leave them

for today. I fancy a coffee, how about you?" I detected a sudden rush to get me back, was it mission accomplished?

I followed her back through the airlock, got sprayed again and got into the main lift, this one had no pass card, just normal call buttons and it was a lot bigger. There was even a run-around in it, loaded with black bags.

"All the normal station traffic uses these lifts," Terri explained. "You must have come up in it from arrivals." I didn't like to tell her that we had used the walkways.

As we descended, the lift stopped at every floor. People got in and soon we were surrounded; everyone looked at me while pretending not to. It made me nervous and I tried to turn away and look at the lift control panel.

Terri noticed that I was getting uncomfortable and announced me. "Hello, everyone; this is Andi. She's taken the Ucky Strike over." And the mood changed a little. I got various comments, wishing me luck, hating Munro, nice to have an alternative to the diner, that sort of thing. But a couple of the women looked a bit annoyed, the sort of look you get when you're having an innocent conversation with their fella.

I might have been many things but that wasn't one of them, maybe I could get a T-shirt. I already needed one that said 'yes my name is Andi, I'm not a bloke!' Perhaps it should say 'And I'm not after your significant other' as well.

There would have to be some way of earning their trust.

We got out of the lift back on the deck we had started from. "Come on," Terri said. "Let's have a coffee in Munro's diner; wind the opposition up a bit."

I was game for that, we were the only customers and the barista was a different one to the guy who had looked daggers at me on the way out. If this one knew who I was, he never said. The selection of cakes and pastries looked pretty good and I realised that I hadn't eaten since I'd sampled my own efforts, several hours ago. He was friendly enough to Terri and after he made our drinks we sat at one of the tables out of his earshot. She had bought cake as well, and it was as delicious as it looked, even if it was so perfect that it was obviously not homemade.

The whole place felt a bit like Munro's conversation, a bit fake and over cheerful, as if it wasn't quite what it seemed but in some indefinable way. It was all very gleaming and that was the problem; it was almost too good. No wonder they wouldn't allow working men in, they might dirty the fixtures; but since this was a working environment that struck me as commercial suicide.

I sipped my coffee, washing the cake crumbs down and thought of the reception I had got in the lift. "So what's with them, Terri?"

"Who?"

"In the lift, half of them were friendly, the rest not so much."

She nodded. "Ah well it's a reversal, half of them are sort of relieved that Mike's gone, he was always after the next conquest, ladies liked the attention when their men were working or tired from working. He was there, in more ways than one. They might not have all succumbed but they might have wanted to. So they miss him." She drank some coffee and took a bite of cake.

"But now, you see, the boot's on the other foot. You're a single lady, now they think that you'll be a threat, just like their men thought that Mike was. It makes them uncomfortable. Especially the ones that are feeling guilty. And they're all thinking about Mike's book."

"Mike's book?" This was a new one on me, although given what she had just told me, I had a pretty good idea what Mike's book would turn out to be.

"The rumour was that Mike kept a book, sort of an insurance policy, all about his ladies and what they got up to. And a few other bits of juicy gossip he picked up in the 'Strike', pillow talk sort of stuff."

I was right; it was that sort of book, and Mike for all his apparent charm was just another rat, like some sort of Trevor in space! Tina saw my look. "There's a few of the men on here who would love to get their hands on that book, and a lot of worried ladies. And before you ask, I'm not in it. I don't think Lou is either."

"I haven't seen a book anywhere." Mind you I hadn't looked, it wasn't in my bedroom but it could be somewhere else. Maybe it was in the freezer with the man himself.

"It might be just a myth, Mike might have just been saying he had one to keep everyone on their toes, but who can tell, it could be hidden somewhere else, not in the café. Munro could have got his hands on it while the place was empty." She took a deep breath, I wondered what was coming.

"I'm going to be completely honest with you, Andi, please don't take this wrong. If you get a lot of attention, especially from the married men, it might be because of the book, not just because you're attractive and available."

She rushed on, obviously embarrassed, her face and neck had flushed. "And you are, of course. But while they might be genuine, just be careful. Mike thought he had it all under control; remember what's in the freezer. The station can be a very dangerous place; Munro was right about that."

I had been about to get annoyed when she said 'completely honest', in my old world, that was almost a declaration of war. But if you thought about it, you couldn't fault her logic.

"I can handle a few randy men," I said. She smiled.

"I expect you can. And then there's the women, they might not be so obvious, although there's a few who might hit on you."

She flushed again. "They'll probably offer to work for you in the café, so that they can search for the book. Be careful and ask yourself what they're really after."

I thought about Maz and her keenness to help. Surely not her? Terri had recommended her, she had to be alright. And all the others this morning, I had been making a list, pleased that people wanted to help me. Oh hell, it got more complicated all the time.

"So who can I trust then? You said you're not in this book; can I trust you?"

She was just about to answer when Munro himself appeared in front of us. "Good afternoon, ladies," he said. "To what do we owe the pleasure?" He sat at the next table and swung around on the chair.

"The café's full," Terri answered, her face blank, "you can't get a seat anywhere and we wanted somewhere quiet to talk."

I supressed a snigger, "Your cakes are nice," I said, "but they're not a patch on my homemade ones."

Munro might not have been amused but he never showed it.

"Well it would be silly of me to throw you out," he said, "as you're my only customers. They'll be back, I'm sure about that."

"Not if we're cheaper," I said. His face was a picture of pity.

"Do you really think you can afford to drop your prices," he paused, "as low as I can, with all the backing I have?"

He was right, I couldn't compete for long and I had no reserves or other sources of income.

"Even if you have to buy or threaten customers, you can't do it to all of them," Terri informed him. "Some of us are immune to your methods."

He smiled, it wasn't a nice expression. "You're right, Ms Hunter," he said. "But when I learn from my contacts about the lovely Andi's past life, or that of her companion, I'm sure there will be things that they don't want everyone to know, family secrets or suchlike. A word here or there, it might put people off going into her establishment."

So it was going to get nasty then, not a bitchy kind of battle but the up-front male kind. I racked my brains; there was nothing skeleton wise for me. "Bring it on then," I said, trying not to show how worried I was by the apparent reach of Munro, at least I had no family that he could threaten.

"It will be my pleasure," he replied. "Enjoy your coffee. Oh, and get the lights fixed will you? And put that letter 'L' back up. Who wants to go for coffee in a red-light bar that can't even get its name right?"

Terri pulled a face as he walked away. "Don't let it get to you; frightening people to get what he wants is standard procedure for him."

That was all very well, and if it was only me I would laugh it off, but I had to remember that I had Cy to think of as well. It wasn't fair to let Munro dig into his life without him having a say. And potentially, he had more to lose; he, by contrast, had some skeletons.

"Do you want to see the rest of the station sometime?" Terri asked me as I polished off the last of my cake. The flush had gone from her face, now she had imparted her pearls of wisdom.

"I do, but I want to have a serious talk with Cy first. I can't involve him in Munro's games if he's unhappy."

"Sure," she said. "I understand; it's a lot to take in. And it can't have been what you were expecting when you took on the place."

"That's an understatement."

"Tell you what, get back and mull it over with Cy, I'm pretty sure you can trust Maz as well, but that's up to you how much you tell her. I'll come over again when I've finished my jobs tomorrow and if you want we can go and see the bit where the real work happens."

Munro was talking to his barista as we left, he saw us pass. "One more thing, Ms Pett," he said. "Our cakes are made on the farm, my wife works in the bakery; I'll pass on your comments."

I was back on form, after my impressive performance where it didn't matter so much. I was antagonising the one person I needed to keep a low profile with. It was foot-in-mouth time. I wanted to disappear as Terri laughed.

"You'll be taking over from me," she gasped. "The look on his face."

Chapter 12

Terri left me, she had to go back up to the observatory. "Don't worry about Munro," she said. "He dishes it out. It won't hurt him to be on the receiving end. Most people wouldn't dare answer him back."

When I got back to the café, the alleyway was still a long thin disco and the café remained in semi-darkness. And the 'L' was still missing; I kind of liked it like that, especially as I knew it irritated Munro. Little victories they might be but I'd take anything I could get for now.

Cy was sat in the middle of a group of women, about seven of them, and he was holding court, probably a load of bull about his life back on Earth. They were lapping it up, all fluttering eyelashes and fawning gestures. Honestly, it made me sick. Or was it that I was jealous of his easy charm? I had to work twice as hard to get half the effect.

He waved at me. "Hi, Andi," he shouted. "I've got a load of ladies here who'd just love to help us out, and they have some tales to tell as well." They all waved. Oh boy, I was going to love telling him what I had learned.

But first, I was bursting. "Catch you in a minute," I called.

I passed Maz, at the coffee machine. "Hi, Maz. Gotta go to the loo, I need to speak to you in a moment."

"Alright, dear," she answered, she was distracted; looking wistfully at the group clustered around Cy.

I shut my bathroom door and sat down, that was when I found out something else, there was a hole in the wall, or bulkhead, whatever; and I could see into Cy's bedroom. I hadn't spotted that before. Yikes! That meant he could see in here. I looked a bit more closely at the hole, it was in the middle of the panel and looked like it had been drilled, it wasn't fresh, there were scratches and scuff marks all around it, like something had been pushed through it on a regular basis.

I pulled a handful of tissue off the roll, wadded it up and stuffed it into the hole. It was just another strange thing at the back-end of a strange day.

I debated mentioning it to Cy; wasn't there was enough else going on? Things seemed to be piling up, like a snowball set down a mountain, more and more was happening and if we didn't decide what we were doing quickly, we would be carried along whether we liked it or not. I finished, zipped up the boiler suit and splashed some water around, I was getting used to the taps and the technique of getting your hands wet before they turned off.

We were going to have to sit down and sort out what we were going to do. I didn't have a clue; I was so out of my depth that it seemed the easiest thing to do was to run again. But where would I go this time? And would Cy come with me? Of course he would, he had wanted to go since we got here. Trying to look more confident than I felt, I walked back into the café.

"Is he always like that?" Maz asked me, shaking her head. "Those people have the potential to be at each other's throats. Somehow he's got them all around a table talking to each other."

"He does that," I agreed. "He has that magnetism, they're like moths and they can't help themselves."

She smiled. "I hope you don't think it's wrong of me to say but in my experience gay men are often like that." Delicately put.

So she had worked it out, and it was true, certainly of Cy. Women flocked to him, he made them laugh, maybe they felt safe, that they knew he liked them for themselves, there was no ulterior motive with him. "We've had a good old talk," she continued. "You've got a very loyal friend there, you're lucky."

She was right, sometimes I forgot just what a good friend Cy had been, I shouldn't; and I shouldn't make any decision without him. He had the saner business head. And the knowledge that we wouldn't get involved with each other made our friendship stronger. I would have to meet these ladies and then see what he made of them; see who he thought that we could trust.

"Those may be some of Mike's exes," she continued. "No-one really knows for sure, except for Mike and the people themselves. When they all ended up in here at the same time, I thought it would be like a sack full of cats. But they're all getting on; he's even persuaded some of them to wait on tables."

Looking around, everything certainly seemed to be under control, there were still quite a few people in, a different mix; there were no miners for instance. But in their place, there was a scattering of suits eating and talking and it smelt sort of meaty. Lunchtime smells as opposed to breakfast; more baked than fried, if you know what I mean. And then I noticed another thing, there was a woman in the kitchen, check apron, floured arms and her dark hair tied back under a cap. She had a cheerful face, it looked like she knew what she was doing; the trouble was that I didn't.

There was just too much going on in here. I definitely needed to catch up. What I really wanted to do was shout *stop* at the top of my voice and then deal with each thing in turn. It was what they would do in the movies. Then they'd have a song. It wasn't going to happen of course. Instead I tried to work out my priorities.

"Who's that in the kitchen, Maz?" My mind was full of Munro's veiled threats and Terri's trust no-one talk; was I getting paranoid?

"That's Clarissa, she makes all sorts of goodies. She heard you were open and came to see if she could have her old job back. I made the decision, but I ran it past Cy first, I hope that was alright?"

Maz looked as if she wanted to say something else; I remembered that she wanted to talk earlier. We had had the thing about the freezer and there had been my desperate attempts to stop her looking. That would have to wait.

"That's fine," I reassured her. "We need people like her if we're to survive. And people like you," I added. "You've been so helpful today. I, we, couldn't have managed without you."

She smiled. "I've enjoyed it, and I can come back in the morning if you like, it'll be just like old times."

"Yes please, we'll sort out all the wages and stuff tomorrow, if that's OK; I want to keep everything proper." And not just for her, I was sure that Munro would be watching to see that I followed all the rules.

"That's fine; take your time to get adjusted. I'll be off then, dear," she said. "It'll be quiet now and Cy said you were shutting at five anyway." That was hours away yet, I looked at my watch. No, it was half past four. "Where has the day gone?"

Maz laughed. "It's the lack of sunlight," she explained. "You can't work out how time has passed so quickly, without the sky it's hard to calculate it somehow. I expect Clarissa has nearly finished as well. See you at eight." She left; as she passed them she said goodbye to Cy and the ladies. I had to keep her onside; we would have to have that proper talk.

My next job was either to see this Clarissa or face the ladies. Clarissa and the smell of baking won. Cy had the ladies under control, he wouldn't do anything stupid. I wished that I could say the same. I went into the kitchen.

"Hi," said the woman, looking up from whatever it was she was doing. "You must be Andi; Maz said it was OK to make you meat pies and pasties, like I used to do for Mike."

She had gloves on and was clearing up after what had clearly been a mammoth baking session. The oven was open and the shelves and trays were washed. She had filled the cooling racks I had used this morning with an assortment of pies and pasties. I could see fruit topped tarts as well.

So she was another one of Mike's 'helpers', I doubted if Cy had been watching her all the time, had she tried to get into the freezer as well? How could I ask without being obvious?

"Did you find all you needed?" I asked her; that was pretty subtle.

"Oh yeah," she said. "I used to bake here once a week for Mike so I knew where everything was kept. I used your flour and stuff from the dry store and the fridge for the pastry but I used my own meat. I got the fruit and veg from Heynrik. I called him when Cy said it was OK and he brought it straight over. I wouldn't use anything frozen; it's not my style. I mean, the burgers that I'm sure you have in your freezer. Do they have any resemblance to the meat in these?"

She waved a pasty in front of my face. It smelt divine, put like that, she had a point. And I felt my stomach rumble, a burger never did that. At least not before I'd eaten it. I'd only had two cakes all day, about average for me but nothing else had passed my lips.

"Can I have that?" I asked, she handed it over and I held it for a second, the pastry was warm, golden and inviting. I took a bite; it was an incredible combination, real meat, like you never tasted on Earth, thick gravy, onions and swede, a proper pasty. Then the kick of the black pepper, whew! Just for a second I was eight again, surrounded by seagulls, rocky cliffs and there was sand between my toes.

"Is this all…?" I mumbled around the mouthful of deliciousness. She nodded.

"Yes, it's all station produce. Derek and the team do a fantastic job, don't they? As well as the ones cooling down, there's fifty or so in the fridge, that should be enough for a few days, plus I've made a batch of chicken pies and some fruity things."

I finished the pasty off in very quick order, licking my fingers for the last traces of the flaky pastry. Fruity things sounded like a very good plan. My mind was on custard as Clarissa looked at me expectantly. "So, is it OK for me to come in once a week then, like I used to? I'll make you a load of stock. Cy said it would be but I'd have to check with you; isn't he a lovely fella?"

It was a no-brainer. "You bet you can! Oh, and how did you get on with Mike?" I tried to sound casual.

She laughed. "Mike was," she thought, "Mike was a pest, he was interested in more than pies, but I wasn't. My man is all I need. Unlike some I could name I'm content, I'm not looking for extra complications."

She sounded sincere, after today I could relate. I hadn't been looking for complications, they had found me all the same.

"I was sorry when Mike went," she continued. "Not surprised, it was only a matter of time before things caught up with him. Sorry because he was good to me, he gave me a chance to do what I loved. But he was the sort who was always going to have to sneak off in the middle of the night."

Interesting comments, they would need more consideration. I was starting to get a better picture of the occupant of my freezer. And as usual, there was more to it than you might have reckoned.

"With food like that I can out-compete Munro's diner." She pulled a face.

"I offered to make them for him, before I started here, he told me that he had his own supplier, I think it's his wife up at the farm. He was quite rude. He said that I couldn't possibly make better products than their machinery could. He hinted that I didn't comply with the health regulations, which was crap. Mike gave me a chance and I've never had a problem, I'm certified in hygiene and so is this kitchen." I was about to tell her my faux pas but she carried on.

"Maybe I shouldn't tell you this but sooner or later you'll hear it. My fella says that Munro is like King Edward, you know, from history."

I didn't, history was not my strong subject; actually school in general was not my strong subject.

Clarissa saw my blank face. "'Who will rid me of this turbulent priest?'."

Priest? what did priests have to do with Munro? No, I still wasn't getting it.

She put me out of my misery. "This is what he means. Mike has his hard-core supporters, they do what he says without thinking, and then there are those he's got leverage over. He can bend them to his will but he also has a load of sycophants, young people trying to impress him. He would have an idea, mutter it out loud and some of the more gullible would take it as an instruction. Like this King Edward, or King someone, anyhow the name's not important."

She turned and gathered up her things. "It means his hands are always clean. Nothing sticks. I'm off, all the dirty stuff is in the washer. I've cleaned down and done the paperwork. I'll send the invoice to admin like usual." She peeled off her gloves and apron. "See you next week then." She breezed out. I heard her say, "Goodbye, Cy," as she walked into the café.

He must have been lounging by the door. "Alright, Andi?" he said. "Those pasties, I had two."

"Two! You're a pig!"

He grinned. "Well I had to do some quality control, and anyway I'd been cooking all day, it had made me hungry. And you swanned off; I expect Terri and you lunched somewhere nice."

"You said it was OK; clear off, you said."

He pulled a face. "I know, impetuous of me, I didn't realise that after I'd finished frying breakfasts I'd be doing burgers and bloody jacket potatoes. That Maz is a slave driver, but at least we didn't get caught out with nothing to sell. After lunch the novelty wore off. Then ladies started coming in and asking about work. I managed to escape."

"Cy, if you hate cooking that much, maybe we can get a cook, but I need to talk to you properly about what Terri has told me. And we had coffee in Munro's place, to check it out and wind him up."

"It's alright, Andi; I'm just teasing. I've really enjoyed it, ask me again in a week and I might say different though. I had finished anyway, the lunches were over and then Clarissa turned up. I'd have only got in her way. I got loads of gossip from Maz and the ladies, and Maz said that the pie thing was kosher, you weren't here and people had asked if they were going to be back on the menu, it seemed OK."

"That's fine, we're in this together. I want to see these ladies, perhaps you can introduce me."

"Oh, they've gone, they had things to do, it's five and I was going to shut up. I can tell you all about them though. They promised me they'd be back tomorrow, you can meet them then." I bet they would be back; moths to a flame, like I said.

Chapter 13

"I've got a lot to tell you as well, Cy. We need to talk seriously, maybe you were right after all, let's lock up, get the kettle on and sort out what we're gonna do."

I wasn't going to start all-night opening just yet, if ever. As I went to shut the door and drop the shutters a young girl ran towards me, about eighteen, all dark hair and make-up, they obviously had Goths in space. "Am I in time?" she asked, out of breath.

"Do you want coffee? We were just closing." I didn't really want to have to send her to the diner.

"No, I want a job; I was rather hoping I was the first to ask."

"What sort of job?"

"I'm a cleaner," she explained, but looking at her I doubted it. Cleaners didn't have long black and red nails; they would poke through the Marigolds for one thing.

"I wondered if you needed the living quarters cleaning out, you know, laundry and that sort of thing; change the beds, dust, tidy. Or clean tables, anything."

"No, that's fine thanks; I can do it."

"I'm really cheap and I've got references," she was persistent, I'd give her that. "I was hoping that you'd let me." She was almost pushing me out of the way in her eagerness to get inside. I had the sudden aroma of rat, and the sound of pennies dropping all at once.

"Tell me your name," I said standing firm in the doorway as she edged from side to side. "I'll let you know."

"Please say that you haven't got anyone else?" she said, panic in her eyes. "I need the money, I'm Davina."

So this was Davina, Derek's daughter. I wanted her to like me; she had given up her work to look after her father when his world fell apart. Terri must have spoken to her. "Let me get organised, we haven't got anyone just yet, I'll be in touch."

"Thank you," Davina said as I retreated and closed the door on her.

Cy had made a pot of tea and we sat at one of the tables. Looking around I could see that we did indeed need a cleaner; there was a fair bit to do ready for the next morning. I would have to check stock as well and make more stuff, bread definitely. It all felt like too much effort, and with what I had learnt I was starting to agree with Cy. Perhaps we should just cut our losses. He seemed to have changed his mind too, awkward sod!

"Isn't it great?" he said, his eyes shining. "I haven't had so much fun for ages, let's stay!" Oh marvellous, he had wanted to go, I hadn't. Now we had both changed our minds.

"Listen," I said, and I told him what Terri and I had talked about, the baggage that came with the café and what Munro had threatened. And Terri's revelation about the book, but I didn't mention her claim of non-inclusion.

"I can't subject you to that sort of scrutiny, Cy. I've got nothing to hide but…"

He looked annoyed. "You think I've got skeletons, hell yeah. I'm gay; it's part of my furniture but I'm open about it. I don't care who knows. It's not illegal, I'm not predatory or promiscuous and I'm not going to be railroaded by the likes of Munro. If he thinks that'll make me leave, I'll do the opposite, just to mess him up!"

"What about Maz? How did you two get on?"

His eyes shone. "Maz is lovely, we had a whale of a time, she asked me straight out if I was gay. But she apologised for asking first, she's got class. She said she believed in being upfront from the start. I told her about Dave and she hugged me, she said she was fine with people being whatever they wanted to be, as long as they were happy. She had that teacher way of getting information but she's great. And she told me loads about Mike while she was doing stuff after the lunch rush, which, incidentally, we could have done with your help with!" He produced a piece of paper. "Here's what we did for the café." He *was* taking this seriously!

I looked, they had made biscuits and more cakes, taken a delivery from Heynrik, disposed of the garbage, chased the electrician up and it looked like they had made us a fair bit of money. And that was all before Clarissa had turned up and done her thing.

"You've done really well. OK then, spill the beans, what did she say about Mike?"

He drank some tea, keeping me in suspense. "Much the same as Terri told you. Mike was a shameless womaniser; there were a lot of sad ladies when he went. Somehow he kept most of them onside, even the ones he had dumped still liked him, there seemed to be little jealousy between them, you saw them all with me when you came back. They'd all been part of his harem, some more so than others and they've all learned something from it."

I'd seen what he meant from the way they had all been sat around talking, Mike must have had the same knack as Cy, till his luck had run out. "What about the male response to our one-man sex machine?"

"There were a few very unhappy men, the ones that found out. A lot of contrite women; the ones that admitted it. The rest of the men were suspicious and Mike was threatened by a couple of them but it never came to anything serious, women have a way of reassuring men about their fidelity, smoothing things over, don't they?"

"Unless you counted being killed and dumped in the freezer as serious." To me it was obvious, his luck had run out; he had upset one man too many, there had been one woman who couldn't 'smooth things over'.

"Maz said that he had a book, the same as Terri said to you. She said that it had names and all sorts of details about the women. She didn't know where it ended up but she says that a lot of people would love to get their hands on it, to prove things one way or the other."

He had confirmed everything that Terri had told me, added some more information and had had just as effective a day as me, all without running around. But he hadn't met Derek.

"We're gonna have to look for the book."

"I know." He thought for a moment. "It's probably why we have so many volunteers for cleaning duties then, when you think about it."

I nodded. "I started a list of people who seemed desperate for that job."

"Like the one at the door just now?"

I told him about Davina and Derek and her desperation to get in and clean. He reached the same conclusion I had. "Either she's in the book and wants to get it or someone sent her to get it."

Maybe she was in it and wanted to get it before her father found out. I nodded.

"Terri warned me, but she thought that a bloke would be most likely to be after it."

"There'll be more I expect, if the contents are that explosive."

"We'll look for it tomorrow, right now we need to get this place presentable for the morning."

We cleaned tables, swept and mopped the floor, cleaned the washrooms and then I got prepped for baking. Heynrik or someone had rotated the stock in the fridge and the veg racks, not that there had been much left from our first free delivery. The way that he had done it gave me an idea about the freezer and its contents.

"Look," Cy said, "when Heynrik put the new stock in, he separated it from the old with sheets of blue paper."

"I saw that, it's a neat idea."

"He told me that it was date coding, today is blue. He said that it helps with stock control, whatever that is. Anyhow he left us rolls of the paper, said he'd do it for us once but tomorrow it was up to us to make room and put the paper up, I think it's orange."

Brilliant! "Come on, Cy, we're rotating the stock in the freezer."

"Heynrik said we didn't need to use it in there, long dates or something."

"Yes, but if we cover Mike's body bag with the coloured paper, no-one will look underneath it, as long as we keep long-dated stock on top."

"Ah, clever idea," Cy responded. I do get them, sometimes.

It wasn't a fun job but we did it, emptying the contents and spreading the paper over the face down body in its white container. Once he was covered up we rearranged the boxes of food, he was now invisible and hopefully immune to a casual search. All the long-dated stuff we left, the stuff that Cy had used most of for lunches went into the other freezer. Mike was locked away again, out of sight but definitely not out of mind.

"As far as I'm concerned, that freezer is empty," I said. "We just use the other one from now."

I took the key and put it in my bag, with all my personal papers, there was no way anyone was getting in there now, not without a crowbar.

Before I slept I started to read the book about the station. It was certainly a massive feat of construction and a huge enterprise. The rings of Saturn had been found to have large deposits of all the raw materials we were running out of on Earth, stuff that we needed to manufacture electronics and all sorts of other things I would never have thought of. And they were a source of water.

So the station was built, first it was just a mining platform, then they added a processing plant, with an accommodation block perched on the top. Conditions were pretty rough until they got established. Then when the profit started to come in, more layers were added. Governments, who had initially refused to part with any cash to help, saw the potential and the changing world order meant that there was a new spirit of cooperation.

The realisation that we were all in it together had helped push space exploration, and Mars had been colonised under domes for a while before the station was started. The mining outfit then diversified into farming, they bought out a company that had been doing it above the Earth and Mars and used the knowledge they had gained. At first the plan was just to feed the growing population of the mining station, but as they learned more; part of the farm became a research facility. Then they started exporting surplus produce, first back to Mars and then to overcrowded Earth. They leased space to the university for their telescope and that was where we were currently at.

The station was a cylinder three hundred metres across and currently had fifteen decks, four were the farm, then there was a park, then four decks of living quarters and facilities. The mining operation took up the rest, with hangars, workshops and the refinery itself.

The core of the lower decks contained the power plant, as Derek had said it was a big chemical reaction, producing heat and power like a battery, it all sounded a bit complicated but it worked. There was an explanation of how the gravity was produced but I couldn't understand a word of it. If I really wanted to know, Lou or Terri could probably explain it to me in words of one syllable.

There were pages of statistics and a list of dos and don'ts but I was nearly asleep, I'd look at them later. And I'd make sure that Cy read it too.

Chapter 14

I'd set my alarm for 4 a.m. again, we had sold nearly all the things I had made and although Clarissa had provided her pies we still needed fresh bread and more cakes. Lou and Terri had promised to help but we hadn't agreed on anything definite, they had other jobs to do as well. Cy, for all his enthusiasm, wouldn't be up till later so it was down to me.

The alarm went off, without bothering with the lights I reached out and turned my straighteners on; then I headed for the bathroom. When I came back I watched in horror as the bedroom door started to open, a line of dim light grew slowly as it was pushed from outside. Someone was creeping in. There wasn't time to put my boiler suit on; at least I had a vest and some shorts to cover my modesty.

I needed a weapon, and quickly. In the dark I climbed across the bed as quietly as I could, aiming for the red light on the bedside table. I pulled the straighteners out of their stand and crept to the wall behind the door. I knew that a burn from them would make you stop what you were doing and think again. A hand appeared and I struck, jabbing the straighteners down on the wrist, catching it between the hot ceramic plates. I squeezed. Hard.

There was a piercing scream and a sizzle as the fibres of the garment-covered arm melted and stuck to the skin underneath. There was the smell of bacon frying. The hand disappeared, pulling the straighteners from my grip, they clattered onto the floor. I heard footsteps and someone shouting and sobbing in pain as I pulled the door open and ran into the corridor. It was empty.

I headed into the space behind the counter, the café's front door was open, the shutters were up; hadn't we lowered them when we closed up last night? Nothing moved, my maimed burglar can't have had time to get across the floor and through the door, they must be hiding. How the hell had someone opened the locks? Of course, I hadn't changed the codes. I must do that.

The room was in part light from Saturn but there were deep shadows. I flipped the light switches and ran to close and lock the door, hopefully whoever was inside would be trapped, surely Cy would have heard the shouting and was even now coming to help me. I had dropped the straighteners and had no weapons, just my anger. How dare someone try and come into MY place?

As I crossed the floor I heard footsteps to one side. I swung my head. I had a brief glimpse of a black-headed figure approaching, the lack of features making it look sinister; and then I was shoulder-charged. The force of the impact shoved me straight into a table. I bounced off and as I flailed around I grabbed at the figure, ripping off whatever was covering its head. They wriggled clear, pushed me into another table and sprinted for the door. I got up and followed them, puffing with the exertion, I needed to get to the gym, if there was one.

As I peered through the door I caught sight of a figure rounding the corner into the main alleyway. I'd never catch them now and my hip was throbbing where I had bounced off the corner of a table.

"What's going on, Andi?" Cy had appeared, and he hadn't bothered dressing for the occasion either. Just lurid psychedelic boxers and a six-pack. But he carried a ladle.

"They got away," I puffed. "I gave them something to think about." I showed him the mask I had grabbed, black and woollen; it was like a balaclava helmet without the face-hole. "Look," he said, there were short blonde hairs stuck in the wool.

"That's a clue."

Suddenly, it was all too much for me and I started shaking, Cy held me tight and smoothed my hair. "It's OK, Andi," he whispered. "They've gone now, that was some scream they gave, what did you do, come out of the bathroom and give them a thrill?"

That wasn't funny, but it did make me laugh and that helped me calm down a bit.

"I got them with my straighteners." He winced. "I got their wrist between the plates. Their sleeve melted into the flesh. It smelt like bacon."

"Well done you, that'll be sore then! All we need to do is find someone with a crispy fried wrist."

We suddenly found that funny and just stood there, holding each other, laughing like a couple of crazies. I had an idea and struck.

"Now you're up, Cy, you can help me make some stock."

"Bloody burglars!" he replied, but he didn't go back to bed, we locked up again and spent the next three hours making bread and cakes and generally getting ready for the day. We talked a lot about the situation, rehashing all the arguments and in the end we decided it was the best thing to stay. The more we talked about it, and now I saw that Cy wanted to stay, the more I realised that I wanted to solve the mystery and find out who had put Mike in the freezer.

Cy, after his initial misgivings, had decided that he liked cooking, and the buzz of the café. He also wanted stay to spite Munro. "Let him dig," he said. "I'll bet he thinks he can use my sexuality against me. He might be surprised to find that he's out of touch."

We also talked about whoever had broken in. "Maybe they were after the pasties?" said Cy. "Have you counted them?"

"That's not funny; I could have been raped or murdered."

"You're right, I'm sorry. If it wasn't because someone found you irresistible then it must have been about this book."

"We need to find them; we should call security, Cy. They could come back."

He thought for a moment. "Two things before we do that. First, he's in pain, he will be easy enough to identify; we don't need to get him. After what you did, he won't be back."

"He could come back with a gun and shoot me! What's the other thing?"

"Reporting it to security would open a whole can of worms. They might want to search the café, which could be a problem. They might find the book, or the body."

So there were points on both sides, in the end we decided to leave it, I would take my chance with the gun. As Cy pointed out, in all the films, a gun in a spaceship was a very bad idea; no-one would be stupid enough to do that, except me maybe. If that was supposed to be comforting it failed miserably.

We got all the baking done and were washing down; Cy had the sausages on and was ready for the breakfast orders when Maz walked in. She surprised me and I jumped.

"I'm sorry, dear," she said. "I didn't mean to startle you; it was just like old times, me working here you see, so I just used the old code for the shutters and the door without thinking. You really should change them you know. There are a few waiting already but I've not let anyone else in yet."

"That's OK, Maz. I'm just a bit jumpy this morning. I will change the codes," I said. I wasn't going to tell her any more about why. She spotted my limp as I moved about.

"Have you hurt yourself?" she asked, sounding concerned.

"Banged my hip on a table," I answered, it was the truth, or at least as much of it as she needed.

There was a queue, a few more people than the previous day but it was easier to deal with, perhaps I was getting used to it. I found myself checking wrists as I worked, none were suspicious. The same people asked me if I had decided about cleaners and waitressing and I stalled them again, we were managing and I wanted to find the book myself before I let anyone else rummage around. And to be honest, I favoured Davina for the job. I was getting all sentimental, or devious. It must be the station getting to me.

And my hip was getting worse. Terri never showed like she said she would; she had blonde hair.

Chapter 15

After the lunch rush, one by one, Cy's legion of admirers came in and he left me to them. This could be awkward, I couldn't really say, "Hi, I'm Andi, were you getting serviced by Mike, how did that work out for you? Oh, by the way, did you kill him and put him in the freezer?" I would have to try to be a little bit more subtle. Hopefully my big mouth wouldn't open before my brain was ready.

They were a mixed bunch, Mike can't have had a 'type', unless it was female and warm, which was pretty inclusive.

There was Meggie, a sophisticated brunette; she told us that she had tried all sorts of different jobs on the station; she currently worked in the mining admin offices. She was elegant, thoughtful and what my mum would have called 'posh'. She sat in her tailored boiler suit, with the understated trim and drew patterns on the tabletop with her finger as she spoke.

She was with Claire, who I hadn't seen in the group yesterday. She was another brunette who didn't say what she did; she kept glancing around nervously, as if she was afraid of being in the café. I got the impression that she didn't do much. We made small talk, hedging around the obvious topic.

Then three girls turned up at once, they said that they worked night shifts on the farm, processing the produce. One was a short, pale redhead with freckles and every other redhead archetype, the others were blonde and not unlike Lou and Terri to look at, tall and thin. They introduced themselves as Jem, Tania and Becc. Jem seemed sort of spaced out and I wondered if she was on drugs.

"Jem," drawled Meggie, "you'll have to stop sniffing all those chemicals you use on the farm, it's making you seem drunk."

Jem giggled. "You caught me out, but when there's no booze and no blokes how's a girl supposed to get enjoyment?"

"But there is booze," Becc said. "Isn't there, Jem? Let's not pretend. The plant produces so many potato peelings; it would be a shame to let them all go to waste. Of course, the sugar has to be sneaked out from under Derek's nose but he hasn't noticed yet."

There was booze! That was exciting, what did you get from potatoes? Vodka wasn't it? That would do nicely after a busy day.

"What about Heynrik?" Tania said. "I thought you were after him."

I forgot vodka for a second.

"He doesn't like redheads," she complained. "He's more a dark-hair bloke."

"Morgana had dark hair," said Becc and then there was silence. "Oops," she said and my ears pricked up.

Meggie saw my expression. "Mike," she said with a sigh, as if that explained it all, "he might be gone but were all still suffering for the illusion that was Mike. Some of us got over it, some like Morgana didn't." There were murmurings of agreement.

"Some of us worked for him but didn't get involved, like me and Clarissa, but no-one believes us!" was Tania's contribution. She got a few sideways looks for that. "I didn't," she said. I had the feeling that she had been saying it for a while.

"And some got pregnant and had to go back to Mars," added Jem. There was silence for a moment. That went with what Maz had told me, did she mean Morgana was pregnant by Mike and had to go? That would make Heynrik a suspect.

"Anyway, you don't want to hear all about that. What can we do for the café?" asked Claire. "I could do with a job."

"So could I," said Meggie. "I'm a cook who's bored in an office."

She was so wrong, I wanted to know everything, I bet they would have told Cy, perhaps they already had. No, he would have mentioned it. I stayed cool and just smiled.

"Thought you were a lady of leisure," Jem teased, Claire looked sad.

"I wish, Clive has had me locked up since my indiscretion; I'm only allowed out now Mike's definitely gone. He wasn't keen on my coming back in here, but…"

She turned to me. "My husband is a mining foreman, he's very possessive; I managed to convince him to give me another chance." She rolled her sleeve up; the bruises were faint but still there, four of them, like fingermarks.

I suddenly became very angry. With Clive? Sure, but also with Mike and with men in general, taking what they wanted, controlling and never, ever realising or accepting the consequences of their selfish actions.

"I have to behave," Claire carried on, her voice quiet. "He went crazy at first but I've been a good wife, I've apologised and done what I've been told, things are getting better. He said I can have my old waitress job back now that he knows that you're not a bloke, Andi."

The others hugged her and grabbed her hands, I saw again that Mike had been destructive in more ways than one; but this Clive had to be a suspect in Mike's demise. They were stacking up, that was two in the last five minutes.

I didn't know how to respond, so I said the first thing that came into my head. "Of course you can, Claire. You tell Clive to come down and see me if he's that paranoid, you can start work whenever you want to."

"Thank you," she said. "I won't tell him that, it might start him off again. He doesn't like to be questioned. But the way I feel now, after getting out and seeing all my friends, I won't let him behave like that again. If he has another go, I'll do the same back. Then I'll leave him." She sat upright. "That's sorted; shall I start waitressing now?"

"Whenever you like, Claire, finish your coffee first." Clive was definitely going on my list.

~~~~

Heynrik, my other new suspect, arrived with a delivery, and despite promises, we hadn't rotated the stock. "Sorry, ladies," I said. "I have to go and sort this out, give me a minute."

Heynrik was not so pleased; he had to wait while we moved things around in the fridge. "Come on, Andi, give me a break. You'll have to get into the routine; I have lots of deliveries to do." Cy passed him a pasty and he munched. "Bribery will help, is this one of Clarissa's? I've missed these. Take your time."

As he chewed and Cy moved the fridge contents, I studied him. He had an open, honest face, surely he hadn't killed Mike, if he had, and he could come back in here looking so relaxed, then he was wasted delivering food. He should be on the stage. I felt sure that he would be safe enough for a date. He saw me looking at him and got the wrong idea. He blushed. Oh crap, now he would ask me out. And I would say yes, even though I desperately wanted Derek to ask. I blushed too.

I suppose it was fair, whoever asked first went first. No, that was Freudian, which was not what I meant. Had first dibs, no; so was that. Oh shut up, Andi! I changed my thought back to the fridge, he was right, we had had to get ourselves organised. We had remembered to bag up the rubbish but neglected to sort out space in the fridge. The coloured paper actually made it a lot easier.

"Shall I do Clarissa's order regularly?" he asked. "It would help to know in advance."

"Yes please, Heynrik, I'm sorry, we'll try to sort ourselves out." I slipped as I turned, my hip was still painful and I sort of fell into Heynrik's arms. He was strong and held me up easily.

He looked at me; it was that sort of look that said I want a quiet word with you. Here we go!

"Cy, bugger off." He rolled his eyes in mock despair and left us alone.

"Do you fancy coming to the cinema sometime?" he asked. "It's probably not where you're used to being taken for a date but it's all we have."

I had given him enough unintended hints then.

"That'll be great."

"God, you're obvious," Cy said after Heynrik had gone. "Stare at him till he blushes, fall into his arms and get swept off your feet. Poor bugger never knew what hit him."

"My hip's killing me," I replied. "I slipped." I could see that Cy didn't believe me, but it was the truth. Still, I couldn't help feeling sort of pleased, until I remembered Morgana. So much for my list, I was having a date with a potential murderer and Derek would be playing catch-up.

Chapter 16

Next morning I beat the alarm, waking up before 4 a.m. with pains in my hip, the whole length of my leg was sore and every move I made hurt. I inspected myself in the bathroom mirror, there was a large bruise on my hip and upper thigh, it must have happened when our burglar had bounced me into the table.

I rummaged around in my things, there were no painkillers left. I had been taking them yesterday and I must have taken the last ones when I went to bed. Just great! I would have to go to the pharmacy near the diner when it opened. That was ages. Maybe it was open now? I dressed; it took me longer than usual, and hobbled to the door.

Even though it was early, there were people about, the diner was open and there were a few punters sitting and chatting over coffee and food. I could see people eating cakes, burgers and someone was even tucking into a bowl of soup. At 4 a.m.! Then I remembered what the girls had said, everyone kept their own schedules, to some four in the morning was breakfast time, to others it was some other time of day. It made me realise just how inflexible the concept of a 'normal' day made you.

Why was seven in the morning breakfast time anyway? If you had been up all night, it made sense for it to be time for an evening meal. The sun didn't rule our day here; it was just a yellow tennis ball in the distance. It didn't need to rule our day on Earth either, when you thought about it.

The pharmacy was open, manned by a lady in a white lab coat.

"Hi," she said cheerfully as I entered, no mention of the time, maybe to her it was mid-afternoon. "What can I do for you?"

I sat in the chair that was placed by the counter. "I've hurt my hip," I said.

"Can I have a look?" she replied, the badge on her coat said Dr Liz Wells. "Come into the examination room." It seemed a bit unnecessary.

"All I want are some painkillers," I said.

"We'll check you out first," she replied.

I followed her into a room that looked like a fully equipped operating theatre. With her help I took off my boiler suit and she helped me onto a bed.

"Is all this really necessary?" I asked her. "It's only a bruise."

"Can't be too careful, we're on a mining station a week from Mars. If you've damaged the joint you'll need surgery." She manoeuvred some sort of machine over me.

"I'll scan it, make sure the joint and the tendons are alright. Lie still," she ordered and pushed a button on the side of it. I held my breath but of course felt nothing. The machine bleeped and she pulled it out of the way. I tried to move.

"Done. Keep still." She peered at my bruise, poked it with a gloved finger; why do they do that? Don't they realise it will hurt?

"Ouch!"

"Sorry, I wanted to examine the lividity. How did you do this?"

That was the big question, technically I didn't. "I'm a clumsy cow," I said. "I bumped into a table in my café."

"You're Andi, Lou told me about you."

"Yes, that's me." I was getting used to everyone knowing who I was; at least she hadn't said that I wasn't a bloke. Lying here in my undies might have helped her diagnosis.

"Well you must have been going at some speed, Andi. This bruise is deep, if I didn't know any better I'd say you ran into the table, or whatever it was you hit at full tilt."

"I was in a rush," I lamely answered. She looked at me but I was keeping a straight face. "This café lark is all new to me," I said. "I was in a hurry to get things done."

She wasn't convinced. "The 'Ucky' has... had a reputation, it used to supply me with plenty of customers," she said. "And I had to pass a lot of them on to the infirmary. But that was when it served beer. There were a few fights; well, about one a day towards the end, that's why the station went dry. I heard that someone had taken the place over. Good for you, Munro needs a kick up the bum, his prices are a rip off."

"Well I won't be doing much kicking till this hip heals, and there I was hoping for a replacement, maybe in a size ten?"

She laughed. "At least you have a sense of humour, you'll need that here."

The machine bleeped again, making me jump, she peered at the screen. "Results are in, and you're going to... live."

She saw my expression and her face cracked into a grin. "You're fine, it's just a bruise, a bad one though. The bone and all the other bits are OK. Just take it easy for a couple of days. Plenty of short breaks. I can inject painkillers or you can have tablets for the pain."

I took the tablets and said goodbye to Liz, before I left I asked her to come down for a coffee sometime and she said that she would. But only if Clarissa was back making pies. She told me that the infirmary had its own canteen but that she would pass on to all the staff that we were open. She said that it would be nice to have somewhere different to go.

I got back to the café, took two of the tablets and got to work. They were different to the ones I had taken yesterday and worked much quicker. The pain was numbed, but I took plenty of breaks like I'd been told, sitting when I would have stood between jobs. Cy appeared, he was making an effort to get up earlier and help out, bless him. I told him about my visit.

"Oh Andi," he said. "I forgot all about your injury, I thought you were just trying to get into a clinch with Heynrik."

Maz arrived, the day got underway, the morning passed and Terri still didn't appear. I got involved with things and it had almost slipped my mind that she had been supposed to be giving me the rest of the tour the day before. Cy mentioned it while we had our lunch, we sat at one of the few empty tables with Clarissa's pies, the rate they had been selling we would need a lot more next week. We had survived the lunchtime rush again; Cy had been cooking flat out and hadn't complained once. The pain had settled into a dull ache, when it flared up I took more pills.

"I thought that you were meant to be seeing Terri this morning?" he said.

"That was yesterday; I have no idea where she is," I tried not to sound worried. "Perhaps the observatory needed her."

"Do you think…?" he said.

We had the blonde hair in the mask, that and her non-appearance was making me wonder, clearly Cy was doing the same.

"I don't want to, maybe she'll turn up," I was doing what I always did, putting off facing up to a possibly unpleasant idea. We finished our lunch and got back to work. Cy took over from Maz so she could eat and I did the counter, I was getting quite good at multitasking. In between I helped Claire, who was working tables on her first day back.

"Hi, Andi," said Terri, she had sneaked in while I was helping Claire. "Sorry; I'm running a day late, how are you?" It looked like I would have to face up to it anyway; I checked her wrists, clean and unburnt. I almost fainted with relief, it wasn't her. But she was acting a bit subdued, not her usual cheerful self.

"I'm good, I was wondering where you were. Is everything alright?"

She looked distressed. "It's Lou," she said. "She's injured herself. We were down the infirmary all day yesterday. Can I get some cake for her? I can drop it on my way up to the observatory. I'm all behind; I'm afraid that we'll have to do our trip tomorrow."

Oh hell, it couldn't be Lou, could it? Just when I thought it wasn't Terri. I had to see her for myself. "I'll take it, what cake does she like best?"

I had to know if it was her who I had caught with the straighteners.

If that was a potential problem, she hid it. Perhaps she didn't know, she had said she wasn't in the book, maybe Lou was. They might have done the double act but it didn't mean that they were joined at the hip.

"Sure," she said. "She'd love to see you, make sure you take her a big piece with plenty of chocolate. Our apartment is dead easy to find, just go up a level and follow the signs. Apartment 54. We'll do our tour tomorrow, thanks, gotta dash." She left in a hurry.

I put a few cakes in a box and set off; Cy and Maz were holding the fort again, but at least this time they had help from Claire. And we would be shutting at five. I would have to make sure that Cy got out soon or he would be biting lumps out of the furniture, at the moment he was happy but he could change quicker than the wind.

"Just you be careful," he warned me as I boxed the cakes. "If you see a burn on her wrist, make sure you keep door-side of her so you can leg it, if you're not back in an hour I'm coming after you." That was reassuring, although it did occur to me to say that it wouldn't take her an hour to finish me off.

Chapter 17

I found the door and knocked. "Hang on," said a voice and there was the scrape of a chair moving.

Lou opened the door, she was balanced on crutches, her wrist was bandaged as was her ankle. She moved backward, nearly fell and just managed to stay upright; her arms were shaking from the effort.

"What happened to you?" I asked as I put the box down, she hobbled across to it.

"Oh yum," she said, opening the box and changing the subject.

The person I had burned had run away, so their ankle had been OK then, but the wrist was suspicious, as was the short blonde hair.

She sat with difficulty and laid the crutches down. "I hate this immobility," she said. "I'm stuck here till the ankle mends; it'll be at least a week."

I felt safe enough to sit, she wasn't in any fit state to chase me. I should be able to get away from someone on crutches, even though I'd probably fall over my feet and spoil it.

The apartment was spacious and about as far away from my living space as you could get. Although my room was cosy, it was very masculine and I hadn't had time or the things I needed to make it mine. This place was very feminine, not overly girly and pink, just relaxing and welcoming without the signs of male presence. Lots of beautiful artwork adorned the walls. Ornaments and photographs were tastefully displayed on quality furniture.

There was a picture window on one wall, showing the usual view of the heavens, we were turned away from Saturn here but it didn't matter, there was still enough of a view to take the breath away. I relaxed into a deep armchair, facing the view. Lou sat with her back to it; I guess she saw it all day at work.

"What happened," I persisted, she looked at me.

"It's really stupid and embarrassing. I was adjusting the telescope and I got my watch strap caught in the gearing. I couldn't reach to the emergency stop; my arm was getting dragged into the gears."

It sounded terrifying. "I was going to get my arm eaten and I just heaved. The watch strap broke." She waved her hand at the low table in front of her, a mangled watch lay on it. "And when it broke I was off balance and fell over backwards, twisting my ankle."

She pulled the bandage off her wrist; there was a red welt all around the place where her watch strap had dug into her flesh. Lots of bruising and dried blood; I was no expert but it definitely wasn't a burn. There was no fabric in it for one thing.

Relief flooded through me, for the second time in as many hours. I couldn't have taken it to find that Lou was involved with all that was going on. She and Terri were people that I trusted. I decided that I would confide in her, over the cake.

"Is there anything that needs doing, while I'm here?"

"You could make some tea, to go with the cake, if it's not too much like work. The kitchen's over there, you'll see everything." She waved her uninjured hand.

Sure, I could do that, she had helped me and was off the hook. Anyway, I realised that the watch injury was on her left wrist, thinking back I was sure that it was a right hand that I had burnt. The clarity of my memory shocked me, I closed my eyes and it was burnt in my mind, the hand, in a glove, thumb on top.

Burnt in my mind, I grinned to myself; that was the sort of thing that Cy would say.

So I made tea in the apartment's kitchen and we sat and talked. "We've thought about it, we're staying," I announced.

"Good," she replied. "Even though you've got dragged into all our goings-on?"

"Because we've got dragged into them, Cy says the same, we want to solve the mystery now and Munro threatening us has just made us more determined."

"Terri told me what happened, you were brave going into the diner and saying what you did about Munro's wife."

"It was her idea to go in there," I said. "But the coffee was good."

"That's my little sis, always has to stir it up a bit." Her expression turned serious. "He will go through your pasts; it could turn nasty for both of you."

"It already has," I told her about the burglar. Her bad hand went to her mouth in shock, the movement making her wince.

"You must have been scared. And when Terri turned up a day late and told you that I was injured; you thought it might have been me, of course you did."

"That's why I had to bring you the cake, to see if it was you."

"That's brave, but a little stupid."

"Not really, Cy knows where I am, so does Maz. Anyway, turns out you can't hobble fast enough to catch me." She laughed.

"What's your next move?" That was the big question.

"I don't know, apart from finding the book, if it exists. I guess keeping both of us safe, running the café to spite Munro, all of the above."

The door opened and Terri walked in. "Any cake left? You," she pointed to Lou, "have given me so much extra work; I'm going to be up all night, and I was going to the cinema."

Lou had the grace to look sorry. "Leave it," she said, "the cosmos will be there tomorrow, and next week, help Andi, she's the one with the problem."

"What sort of problem?"

So I had to tell it all again. At least this time Terri made the tea.

"But that's awful," she said as I described the figure running away. "You should call security."

"But what if they search the café? They might look in the freezer?"

Lou nodded. "That's true, and if it was Munro he might have done it to give them a reason to search."

"Someone told me he was like King Edward; I didn't really know what they meant."

Lou nodded. "Who will rid me of this turbulent priest? That's perfect, I'd never thought of him like that before."

Terri nodded, grinning. "Perfect, except it's actually Henry II."

I was still in the dark. "I don't care which king it was, can you please explain about this bloody priest, and humour me for a moment. I went to a convent, I was taught about loads of priests but I don't remember a turbulent one."

They were both rolled up laughing by this time, what had I said?

"OK," Lou said. "Henry II appointed someone called Thomas as his Archbishop of Canterbury."

"I'm with you so far." Then they went into rapid 'let me finish your sentence' mode. My neck ached from turning to each as they spoke.

"The story was that Thomas criticised Henry, he was his friend but he overstepped the mark."

"One day Henry had had enough of Thomas's criticism, he was the king after all, he muttered 'who will rid me of this turbulent priest', or something like it."

"He was thinking out loud and fed up with him going on and pointing out his flaws; some knights heard him say it and thought it was an order."

"So they went and killed Thomas, believing they had done what the king wanted."

"Even though it wasn't." I got a word in edgeways.

"Probably wasn't. Anyway, Henry said after that he hadn't meant for it to happen, that his hands were clean of Thomas's blood."

Ah, it was all clear to me. "So Munro can mutter, 'I wish someone would burgle Andi's bedroom', and some bright spark thinks it's a job. Afterwards Munro says, 'I was just thinking out loud, nothing to do with me'."

"Exactly," said Lou. "Got it in one."

"We should have been teachers," Terri said.

Exhausted by the effort of trying to educate me they drank tea in silence for a while.

"We know we should be helping you in the café," Lou said. "We did promise after all."

"Don't worry too much, I know you have other things to do, your real jobs for instance. Anyhow, Lou, you have to get better before you can do that."

"Give me a week," she said. "As soon as I can stand without the crutches I'll make you some cakes, I can drag out my return to the observatory for a bit."

Terri made a noise at that suggestion, Lou turned to her.

"Terri, you're not to do extra for Welkson, that's our boss, Andi, just because he says so. He's always making you feel guilty to get you to do more work."

"I wish I could stand up to him like you do," she muttered.

"Well do then, you're not a slave!"

Sisters! I felt uncomfortable and tried to change the subject. "Anyway, you have helped; after all you got us Maz and our first day's customers. They're all coming back now and bringing friends and that's great. Clarissa is making pies and Claire is working for us. None of that would have happened without you."

Chapter 18

The next day I had a lie in, well, until six. The burglars were having a day off as well. Cy and Maz had done a load of baking while I was with Lou and we had little to do. Terri had promised me that we would go and visit Tina but I was feeling guilty. Cy was getting left out, he hadn't been out of the café since we had arrived. My hip felt a lot better, I had slept well and didn't bother taking any more tablets.

"Don't you want to have a look around?" I asked him. "I'm off gallivanting every day and you're stuck here. I feel bad about it."

"It's fine," he assured me. "You go on sleuthing, I know you love it. I'm getting into the whole café thing and I'm enjoying the change. Besides, sightseeing isn't my idea of fun, I can listen to the gossip here and Maz is great company. Everyone is so friendly."

It made me feel better to know he wasn't feeling left out. "You'll have to go and explore, Cy," I said. "If you've read the guidebook, there's a gym and a park and all sorts." His expression showed me that he considered those things 'boring', and that he obviously hadn't read the book. Ah well, if he was happy, I would just carry on. One thing with Cy, if he stopped being happy, all the station would quickly get to know about it.

"You should read the book, Cy. Go and see what's out there," I tried again. "I've seen some amazing stuff since I've been here."

"Yeah, yeah," was all he would say.

Terri arrived mid-morning. She looked tired, her face drawn. "Come on then, let's take you down to the mining deck."

"Are you sure? You look like you've been up all night."

"I'm OK, just an early start and a lot of concentrating. I took

Lou's advice and went to the cinema last night, then I had hot chocolate and a good gossip with the girls. It was late by the time I got to sleep. Hey, you should come with us next time, it'll be fun."

A girls night out sounded like a great idea, as long as we didn't talk about Mike, Heynrik, the book, Munro, violent husbands or any number of other things.

"I was going to do Lou's stuff but I thought sod it. Lou's right; I shouldn't be a doormat for Welkson. It's mostly duplicating to confirm findings anyway. I want to go down to the workshops, if nothing else; I haven't seen Tina for ages. And I did promise to take you down there."

"At least have a coffee before we go."

We sat and chatted. "After you told us about your intruder," Terri said, "I went and had a look in our gear locker, in the observatory lobby. One of our hats was missing."

Hats, when was it ever cold enough for a hat?

Terri saw my look. "When we go to the telescope at the base of the station, it's turned away from the sun permanently and we can't heat it cos of condensation on the optics. Seriously, it gets bloody cold down there."

I never realised that. "Who could get in and take it?"

"Well, it's only accessed by the secure lift so in theory only a few people, the trouble is that I don't know everyone who has access. But I can find out, the control room will have the key-card logs. That's a job for when I'm not so busy."

"How's Lou this morning?"

"Her ankle is better, it's just a sprain, she'll be OK in a few days. The wrist is sore, she's really lucky though, someone lost an arm last year. We asked for guards on the machinery but Welkson says that the extra metal would screw up the magnetic field on the other sensors in the room."

Was that really more important than someone's arm?

"Can we stop off at the admin centre; I need to chase the electrician, and there're a few things to order."

"Sure, but I'll bet Munro has put the word in to delay it."

"It was him who reminded me to get it done, you were there."

"Yup, that's his way, he'll get you chasing round in circles till you think you're going crazy."

We drank up and left, walking past the diner, it was still empty; we got in the main lift and went down a deck. This was familiar territory; this was where we had arrived. Was it only a couple of days ago?

Beside the arrivals hall was a large glass frontage, 'Station Administration' it said over the door. Inside, through the glass I could see a row of people sitting at terminals, typing and talking. Off to one side there was a line of people.

"The queue's not too bad today," Terri remarked as we joined the back. "Admin can't have messed up quite as much as usual."

I needed to arrange for the lighting to be fixed, and there was the matter of a regular garbage collection as well. Heynrik was taking the food waste but there were other bags of rubbish. Plus there were some things we needed; I'd been keeping a list.

We moved slowly up the queue. In front of us was a partition and behind it a harassed looking woman with cropped black hair. She had the haunted look of someone who was the receptacle for everyone's woes, without the power to do much about any of them.

"She looks happy in her work," I remarked as the line shuffled forward slowly.

"Long story, you haven't been here long enough to see how things work, or rather don't. I'll tell you about her later."

That was comforting, we were in a bubble in space, if the slightest thing went wrong we would all die and it was badly run!

I could hear her conversation with the man in front of us. He needed some things from Earth and she was trying to keep calm as she explained why they could not be instantly produced. "The shuttle takes a week to come up from Mars, sir," she said for the third time. "And when did you order the items?"

His reply was indistinct, but I got the impression that he expected the laws of physics to be broken for him personally. Or at least modified.

Terri whispered in my ear, "That's Zeke; he grows flowers and vegetables up on the farm. His wife was one of Mike's cast-offs, when he found out it sent him a bit crazy. He took her back and now he buys her loads of expensive things all the time, almost like bribes to make her stay."

It was sad to see it, so many lives ruined and for what? A poke, and a prime place in the freezer, under the burgers.

He departed, head down, muttering and it was our turn, "Yes," said the woman, "where are you from?"

"The café," I said. She looked dubious, "There's a café? I know about the diner but I didn't know there was a café as well."

"Mike's old one," replied Terri and her face brightened.

"Oh you must be Andi," she smiled. "With the name we all thought you were another bloke." She almost sounded relieved. "What can I do for you?"

"I need some lights fixing, garbage removed and a few stores," I said, getting my list out.

"Let's have a look," she took my list and pushed it into a slot on the side of her desk. It disappeared. What was happening? There was a noise and it emerged again; I thought for a moment that she had trashed it.

"Scanned it," she said, handing it back to me and looking at her screen. "Now then; I can get you an electrician and garbage removal tomorrow, and most of the things you want are in stock in the commissary. We can deliver them by run-around when you open in the morning. Shall I put them on your account?"

My account, I had an account! That was going to be my next question; I thought that I would have had to open one. Munro had mentioned it. She tapped at her keyboard. "Yes the Ucky Strike still has an account here, for this sort of thing." She punched more keys and a stack of paper presented itself. "You haven't had a print-out for a while, since before Mike left in fact. You seem to have been busy though, here's your current statement."

That was a surprise, Mr Greasy had never mentioned that I wasn't starting from zero, the number was small but at least it wasn't red. And did everyone call it the Ucky Strike? Perhaps I would leave the 'L' in the store.

"And this is all mine?"

"You're the leaseholder; the money stays with the concession owner. So as long as you're up to date with the rent, yes it's yours; it's takings less deliveries, and the last tenant left a small balance, which I've carried over. As you must've noticed there's no cash on the station, all the transactions are electronic; this is an up to the minute real time figure."

I looked more closely at the last sheet; Mr G had put my 400 cash through the system, in and out, the first delivery from the farm was shown as no charge. I would have to check it all out properly but it seemed like my worries over accounts were unnecessary. It was all done for me. Things were looking up.

Chapter 19

We went down another deck. "This is where the real work starts," Terri said. "The only reason the station's here. Everything else is here because of the mining operation." I wondered if anyone had told Derek and the rest of the farmers.

We stepped out of the lift into bedlam. There were people running around and shouting, the smell of grease and small clouds from the welding and burning of metal drifted around. Flashes of light lit up the space with harsh shadows above the normal lighting.

"Keep to the yellow path," Terri advised me, it stretched out in front like the way to the Emerald City. This was what Tina had meant, a safe walkway through the workshops. Just like the markings on the deck that the run-arounds were supposed to keep to. We went past all sorts of craft, some like bulldozers, others with cranes and hydraulic arms fitted.

Then there were the really weird ones, mind you they all looked weird to me. They were scarred and battered; there were dents all over them despite the rubber fenders liberally scattered across the hulls. The glass panels were all covered by a thick mesh; protection I guessed, although it could have been for any reason, spaceship design wasn't really my strong point. People were working on them, crawling underneath, removing panels and working on engines, it all looked totally random. As I watched, one rose up out of the deck. "Lift from the hangars," shouted Terri above the din.

Tina must have spotted us as she wandered over; she had thick leather gloves on and a welder's helmet tipped back. The shorts had been replaced by a stained blue boiler suit.

"Hey, you two, so you've come for a visit? Welcome to the

madhouse. Come on over to my bench."

We left the yellow path and I tensed, ready to be hit with an insult or at the least a piece of flying metal. But nothing happened as I reached the safety of her workbench. There was a jumble of metal objects on it, she picked two of them up and clipped them together with some sort of clamp. The place was nowhere near my idea of fun, all greasy and with an undertone of sweat and excess testosterone, more like a broken nail shop than a workshop.

"What are you all doing?" I asked her. "It looks so chaotic."

"Fixing the mining craft up after the miners have spent all day breaking them," she replied. "I'm forever welding fenders back on or patching leaks. And are they grateful? What do you think." She waved her welding gun thing at me. "Do you wanna have a go, Andi, see if you can join these bits up?"

She put the pieces of metal in a vice on the end of the bench. It would have been an irresistible challenge to ninety-nine per cent of males; I could just about live without it. But I didn't want to be rude. I shuffled about.

"Me? Weld?" I tried to make a joke out of it. "You have to be joking, I can't stick bits of metal together." I couldn't even stick with Trevor back on Earth.

"Go on, Andi, try something different." Terri pushed me forward. Cow! I stumbled and grabbed the bench. Taking advantage of my flailing hand, Tina thought that it was enthusiasm and shoved the bloody welding thing in it.

"That's the way, hang on while I put a visor on you," she crammed the helmet over my hair. It was dark in there. She took my hand, and swiped it at the things in the vice.

"Keep hold and let me move the torch," she said. Suddenly it wasn't so dark, there was a crackle and I could see through the tinted visor of the helmet; blow me down, was I welding? I was; I was actually welding! Strangely, it felt good, as long as no-one would be relying on it for anything. "I'm letting go of your hand," Tina announced. "Just keep the gun moving along the groove, slow and gentle."

I did, until I got to the end. "Well done. You're hired," Tina said as it went dark again. "A bit of training and you'd be fine."

"Who's this, Tina?" a deep male voice boomed out behind me, I turned, straightened up and lifted the visor.

"Hey boss, this is—"

"Andi," I finished, wrestling my way out of the helmet.

"Hello," he said. "You're the one who's taken over from Mike?"

"Yes, that's right." I was getting used to this, I knew what was coming next; bet he said that I wasn't a bloke.

"So the rumours were right, you're not a bloke." He was observant, I'd give him that, maybe it was the boiler suit; the fitted shape and the absence of a T-shirt did little to disguise my curvy bits. That and the big hair, messed up by the helmet it must have looked like a portable jungle perched on my head.

"This is Chandler," Tina announced. "He's the mining company representative on the station, so technically he's in charge of everything."

He was a big man, muscled shoulders and lithe in a white shirt and smart trousers. Not my type though, there wasn't that spark. Nothing to do with the fact that he looked more like an estate agent than the man in charge of the operation.

"Everything except me," Terri solemnly suggested.

"We're not having this argument again, Terri," he answered with a smile. They liked each other then, he must have been her type.

My arrival had drawn a crowd, I realised as I looked around me. There were about twenty people stood watching. One of them, an ugly faced man with lank hair and stud earrings spoke up. "Chandler, what's that tart doing down here?" There were murmurs from the other men.

Well that was rude and I saw Tina colour. She walked over to the man and stood about an inch away from him. "She's my guest, Clive, and if you don't like it, don't stand there watching, get back to wherever you were skiving just now. There's no need to embarrass her."

"Shut it, Clive," Chandler added.

So this was Clive, I could see the belligerence in his face. Even though I had never met him, he had already made me angry. I had seen the results of his attitude on Claire's arm and decided to stick up for myself. I dropped the welding gun and walked over towards him, Tina stood aside. He was about a foot taller than me and he sneered as he looked down.

"So you're Clive, I've heard all about you," I started. "Do your friends here know what you get up to?"

"Don't know what you mean," he blustered; his eyes fixed about a foot below my chin.

"Lift your face up, they aren't talking to you." There was laughter. He tore his gaze away and looked me in the eye.

"Now I've got your attention, if you don't want me to tell them how brave you really are, I suggest you shut your noise." I couldn't believe that it was me talking, I normally shrank from confrontation. But I'd seen the fear on Claire's face, this was a bully and for the first time in my life I had decided to stand up to one.

He went red. "That bitch been moaning to you has she, you know nothing, she made me look stupid, chasing after him, just cos he was nice to her. And you're a fine one to talk, with your tame queer. Can't you get a real man for yourself?"

That was enough; I wasn't having that said about Cy, especially behind his back by a wife beater. And I probably could get a real man, if I could find one around here. I turned and walked away, fighting to contain my anger.

"Go on then," he jeered, "walk off when you can't take it."

I looked at Terri, she had gone pale and when she saw what I was doing, she shook her head.

I stopped by the bench and picked up a large hammer. Clive had taken his eyes off me and was laughing but the others hadn't stopped watching. As I moved back towards him, holding the hammer, he realised what was happening and panic set in, his face fell as he saw my expression. He tried to run but his mates stopped him. Typical bully, stand up and they try to melt away.

"Do you want to tell me where the real men are then?" He was silent.

Chandler came and stood between us. "OK, that's enough. I'll take that," he said, removing the hammer from my grip. I was pleased, it was bloody heavy and I'd been desperately hoping that I wasn't going to have to use it. I would have had a go though, and I think that most of the group realised it. And swinging it could have landed me on my arse.

"What's the matter, Clive?" someone shouted from behind him. "Not used to someone answering back?"

"Or is it too public?" another voice shouted. There were more laughs. He slunk away.

"There'll be a lot of happy men around here now, and your place will be filled with them once word gets around," said Chandler. "Everyone will know that you stood up to Clive, he's full of shit. Don't worry; you scored a lot of points there. Between them Clive and Mike had been the bane of my life. Clive's just a bully, he talks a lot; argues about everything and stirs it. Stand up to him and he'll fold, like you saw. Mike was a pain, with his antics he did more to disrupt the mining than all Tina's dodgy welding."

She punched him on the arm, he laughed.

"Now all you have to worry about is the miners thinking about hitting on Andi instead of them thinking about Mike hitting on their wives," said Terri helpfully.

I sort of understood what she meant. "I'm not here to encourage anyone," I started, he laughed.

"None of the blokes here need any encouragement; they can manage on their own. Anyway, the word will get round, no-one's gonna mess with you after that." I might not have fancied him but I liked him.

"Has Tina asked you out yet?" he said. What! Was Tina…? I did a double-take. Terri grinned.

He must have seen the shock on my face. "On a Scooper," he said. "For a trip, course you'd have to go on the simulator first, make sure your stomach's up for it."

"Your comic timing's lousy, boss," Tina said, red-faced.

He laughed. "That was for the punch."

Me? Go out there? Last week I'd have run a mile, now it seemed like a natural thing to do. That and the view from the observatory had made me want to. And I was being offered the chance. Why not? I'd surprised myself already, standing up to Clive like that, I might as well go for it.

"Sure, I'd love to."

"Tina can set it up," he said. "She has to fly her own repairs, we think of it as a sort of incentive system. And she's an instructor. Get her on the sim, Tina. I'll tell Don in the control room that it's OK and leave it to you to sort it out."

Tina smiled. "I thought I'd be taking Cy on the simulator before I took you. He seemed keener than you did."

"That's all show, you won't get him out there; Cy feels sick watching things moving on the TV, whatever he says." I knew, I had listened to his barfing all the way from Earth, via Mars.

"Yeah but Cy's cute," Terri joined in, she had given me several thoughtful looks since I wielded the hammer, maybe her opinion of me was changing. "Come on, let's get you back to the café, I'll bet you that the news of your adventures gets there first."

As we walked through the workshops, Terri was close to me; there was something about her, she moved differently, was it because of what I had done, or because she had seen Chandler?

"I thought that was a bit unfair," she said as we entered the lift. "After all Cy's just a bloke, calling him your tame queer was out of order, I'd have gone for him as well except you beat me to the hammer."

I wondered if she would, she sometimes seemed to be strong, sometimes not. We stood side by side in silence, and then Terri turned to me. "Listen," she said intensely, putting her hand on my arm, "if you find the book, and I think you will, you'll see that I lied, I am in it."

"Oh hell." That was a shocker, I put my arm around her. "Terri, I'm not in the business of telling the world, or whatever you want to call this place, I only want it to get it off my back. If I can prove it's gone, or never existed, perhaps people will leave me alone."

She looked less worried at that. "I'm not in it for what you think, I might not be in it at all. I'm in it because of what I wouldn't do. I told Mike to get his hands off of me when I was working in the café. He didn't so I slapped him."

She faltered, her eyes moist. Interesting; so Mike could be vindictive as well as a charmer, I got the feeling that there was more, but that she was afraid how I would take what she was going to tell me. Whatever I had done in the workshop had made up her mind that I could be trusted. What had I done that had been so special?

Chapter 20

I was sure that she was about to tell me as the lift door opened, but she never got the chance. As we walked down the alley amongst the people wandering about I spotted one with a bandaged wrist, walking away from us towards the diner. "There," I shouted to Terri, waving my hands. "There, with the bandages." The person heard me shout, looked round and legged it. I moved towards them and almost got run over for my trouble. There were people everywhere, it was afternoon shift change and I could barely keep track of the figure, it was definitely male as its head bobbed and people scattered.

When the run-around passed, I saw the figure heading down a side alley, not the one that led to the café. I ran after them and could hear Terri follow. They had a good lead on me and I had to shove a few dawdlers out of the way as I followed the alley. It went around a couple of corners, the sound of running footsteps receding. The alley ended at the outer wall of the station. Where had they gone? I hadn't passed any doors, there was nowhere to go. Terri arrived beside me; she was puffing a lot less than I was. I leant on the rim of a port, gazing out at Saturn. It had seen where the man had gone, but it wasn't letting on.

"He must have gone up the auxiliary stairs," Terri panted. "Come on." She pressed a button where the panels met, I could hardly see it, a door swung open. I could hear the clang of feet above us as we started to climb. Behind us the door closed. There were no ports in the stairwell, only harsh fluorescent tubes, throwing weird shadows. The stairs were made of metal strips, I was in the lead. Looking up I could see the shape of a man moving past the lights.

We went up a level, then two. I was slowing down and I knew that he was getting away. We got to the park level, the sound had stopped. He must have left the stairs somewhere. Or he was above us and keeping quiet. I looked up through the stairs; there was no sign of anyone above me. Surely I would hear his breathing.

Terri arrived. "I need the gym," she said. "I've not moved so much since the time I was telling you about, when I tried to get away from Mike's wandering hands." That was enough information for me and we alternately laughed and puffed as we stood holding onto the handrails.

"Did you see who that was?" I asked her.

"One of the farmworkers I think, but I couldn't swear to it."

I thought that I had seen him somewhere before too, the thing was the only person I had seen on the farm was Derek, and that wasn't him.

"Now we've ended up here and it's quiet," she said, "I can tell you the rest of my awkward moment."

"Go on then," I encouraged her.

"Promise you won't tell anyone else, not even Lou." Her eyes looked wild, the lighting made her face look like a mask of fear, what was she so worried about?

"Of course I won't, I'm just not the sort to kiss and tell," I thought that would be reassuring; instead it made her do a double take.

"I did wonder," she said, "when I realised that Cy was gay, whether your partnership was a... you know... convenience thing."

Oh boy had she got it wrong. "It's not like that at all," I said. "We both had partners back on Earth and we both got dumped on, me more than Cy, I think he was just bored with Dave. Anyhow when I left, he decided to come with me. We're not one of those lavender relationships if that's what you're thinking."

"I thought I must have been imagining it," she went on. "You showed me today that you understood, you were willing to stand up to Clive, because you respected Cy's lifestyle, I thought then, I can tell her."

What was I now, an agony aunt?

"Go on then, Terri."

She took a deep breath. "Mike had his hands all over me in the storeroom and the truth was that I didn't mind it that much. But it was all just so sordid, so presumptuous, he already had a reputation by then, I wasn't the first on his list by any means." She stopped. "You promise that you won't tell anyone don't you?"

"Of course not, Terri," but I was starting to wonder if her next words weren't going to be, 'I killed him'.

"When I told him to leave me alone, that I wasn't interested, he said that I must be the only one on the station who wasn't, he asked me if I was only into girls."

Smug bastard, what was it with the men who thought that they were irresistible? If you didn't fancy them you were frigid or a lesbian.

Terri said what I was expecting. "He said I would have to go into his book, that as I was the only one who had resisted so far, that there must be something queer about me." She started to cry and I hugged her.

"'Oh well', he'd said, 'I'll just have to make some rumour up, something really sordid, to keep my reputation'. That really hurt me, I ran out, straight into Maz."

There would be no hiding from Maz, her teacher sense would pick that up without getting out of first gear.

"She looked at me and asked me what the matter was, I told her everything and she was really annoyed.

"'You can be what you want, dear', she said. 'And it doesn't matter what he thinks'. She said that he had told her she wasn't bad, for an older lady."

I could imagine her reaction. "What did she say to that?"

Terri was calmer now and her smile had almost returned. "She said, 'I told him he'd never find out how bad, or good I was, I was more partial to girls and I'd write that in his bloody book myself if he wanted'."

I had to laugh; Maz had burst his bubble in the best possible way.

"But I'm still worried that I'm in the book and that Lou will find out, believe it and hate me." And I knew what she meant, when a sister hates you, then that really is the end of the world.

"Look, Terri," I said to her, "I promise you, if I do ever find the book, that page will be the first in the disposal, don't worry." She smiled and hugged me for a moment.

"Thank you," she said.

"Come on, let's get back." We left the empty stairwell and rejoined the bustle of the station.

Chapter 21

Now we had even more reason to find this book. After Claire and Maz had gone home and we had shut up for the night, I lowered the shutters and locked them from the inside. I had changed the code as well. Then I retreated and locked the door.

Between us, Cy and I proceeded to take the place apart. I reckoned that the best place to hide it would be where no-one in their right mind would leave it, so I concentrated on the storerooms and the kitchen; he thought it would be in some sort of secret place in the private accommodation. I told him to keep the hell out of my room; he said my undies wouldn't fit him anyway.

I realised that I was in the wrong place when I left the kitchen and moved into the dry store. There were so many places that a book could be left, in boxes of stock, in a bag in the flour sacks. I couldn't reach half the boxes, let alone move them. I just stood for a moment and thought 'this is impossible'.

I realised that I had to be smart; I had to think like Mike; where would he consider it a safe place to hide something this important, something that no-one else would see. The flour and baking stuff I discounted, Clarissa would be using it weekly and she might find it. Likewise the veg store and the fridges. Oh hell. The fridges; we had binned all the stuff from the fridges but we hadn't searched it first, what if the book had been hidden in a container in amongst the cheese or butter?

The trouble was, you could make a case for and against hiding it anywhere. Maybe it wasn't even in here; maybe Mike had a trusted friend who kept it. This was hopeless; I just hoped that Cy was having more luck.

I looked through a few boxes but my heart wasn't really in it, then I heard Cy shout.

It was a triumphant howl from the direction of the spare bedroom he was using as a gym, and I left the stores and rushed in. The room stank of the cheap scent that smelt OK on him, but in the air on its own had the aroma of lavatory cleaner. The drawers from the chest were on the floor and a book was in his hand. An innocent looking leather bound thing, it had a hasp and a lock.

"Where did you find that?"

"Taped under the bottom drawer," Cy explained. "Oldest trick in the…"

"Book?" I suggested.

He nodded. "Now we need to find the key."

I looked at the lock; it was a tiny little thing, more for show than anything else. In all likelihood the key would be in the freezer, attached to the body of its former user, failing that, it could be anywhere. I didn't fancy searching the body, anyway we would have to empty the freezer; there was, however, a quicker way.

"I know where I've seen a key that'll open that," I said, Cy looked mystified. I went to the kitchen and came back with the largest knife I could find.

"Here it is," I said as I sliced through the leather.

Cy cringed. "That's sacrilege."

"Would you rather search for it? Perhaps it's on the body, or in the bottom of one of the flour bags. Maybe it's frozen in a tub of ice cream."

"Good point, well made; your key is so much better."

I opened the book, expecting chapter and verse on one man's rampage through the female inhabitants of the station.

Blast! It was in code.

Cy peered at the pages over my shoulder; there were columns of letters with numbers randomly interspersed. Each page had a title, but they were in a code as well. I flicked through the pages, every page had a title and every title was exactly ten symbols long.

"Who can we trust to work this out?" he mused.

"I'd rather not tell anyone we found it. What about you, Cy, can't you decipher it?"

"Looks a bit beyond me," he admitted with a frown. It was all a mixture of letters and numbers, pages and pages of it, all in five letter blocks, neatly spaced in columns. "I wouldn't know where to start."

"What shall I do with it then?" I was all for destruction.

He replied without hesitation, "Hide it again, somewhere else. Then let's pretend that we never found it, for a while at least, until we can make a copy of it."

"What good will that do us?"

"I'm thinking, Andi; we know a bit about the way things are now and we don't want to start involving anyone else in it. Lou and Terri might be the obvious choice for helping us to decode the book," he said, "but I don't want to involve them, even if they have the brains, and according to Terri they're not in it."

As he said that I remembered my conversation with Terri, I didn't want to repeat that. Cy was right though, we couldn't involve anyone else. This one was down to us. Cy went on.

"We can't know what it might say, if we get someone on the station to help us, the first thing they read could be about them, or someone they know."

"That's true," I agreed, desperately trying to think of a solution while Cy piled on the reasons to do it ourselves.

"We don't know what they'll find, or how loyal they are to whoever it was that was being written about." They were all good points.

"You're right then," I said. "We can't trust anyone."

He sighed. "I'll have a look. It can't be too complicated as it's handwritten, it's probably based on his birthday or something similar. If it was on a computer it would be a lot harder to break."

"How do you mean?"

"Well, he has to be able to write it without notes, so it'll be a letter substitute or addition, something that's easy to do once you get the hang of it but enough to foil a casual look. Like I said, we really need to make a copy, so I can write notes and try things without damaging the original."

And with that thought, I went to bed, it had been another full-on day. I could do with a break.

Chapter 22

"We could really do with a day off." Cy had read my mind.

We'd hidden the book in my room, under the bedframe in my suitcase, with some of the clothes that I wouldn't need now that I was wearing boiler suits all the time. It wasn't ideal but it was different, if someone thought that they knew where it was and came to get it they would be disappointed. They might not think of looking for it in amongst my gear. For all they knew we hadn't found it.

"It's a nice idea, Cy, but how are we gonna do that?" It was a little after six and we were making stock. Cy was now in the routine of getting up early, he was really enjoying himself, for the first time in years. He had lost weight and was exercising with the gear he had found in the spare room. He was talking about going to the gym, meeting people and getting involved. Maybe he had read the guidebook.

"Just don't open, put a sign up," he suggested.

"Or we could leave Maz in charge." I didn't want to lose the goodwill we'd been building up by randomly shutting. That would only help Munro.

"Maz needs a day off as well; she's been here every day since we opened. She must have a life outside the café."

"We'll tell Maz today then and shut the café tomorrow."

Maz took the news really well, she smiled in that teacher expression they pull when you finally realise what's going on. "I was going to mention it to you," she said, "because I'm not going to end up coming in here every day myself. I wondered how much longer it would be before you worked it out."

"Fair enough; we appreciate your help, Maz."

"I know you do," she said. "I'll tell everyone today that your closing one day a week starting tomorrow, and don't forget, you still have the list for some extra help if you wanted to have a day off and stay open."

That was true, now we had the book and it was in a more secure location, apart from the freezer there was no reason not to let anyone work here. And I had a few ideas about that too. Meggie had mentioned that she was a cook and Davina was keen to clean for us, if we were making enough cash maybe we could afford to employ them and have a bit of time off for ourselves. I would have to check the books and discuss it with Cy.

Then, around mid-morning, it all kicked off, there was an ugly atmosphere developing, I could feel it. One of a group of four miners, one that I didn't recognise, was muttering about Mike's love life and what he imagined had gone on in the café. He had clearly been stewing for a while, his mates were telling him to be quiet but his voice escalated until we could all hear it. Then he said the name 'Julia'. The whole place fell silent.

I looked across to where Julia was sitting, she was one of the regulars and a quiet girl, she wasn't one of the ones who had asked for a job and seemed to have no past. She came in, had coffee, knew a few people and that was about it. She was sitting and talking with her friends. I could see that she had gone red as the loud voice described what he imagined her and Mike doing while some bloke called Jeff was out earning money in a Scooper.

"And another thing," he finished off, "whilst she was in the back with her legs wrapped around that bastard, Jeff was so fed up with it all that he drove into a rock. Full speed. And all because he couldn't take what she told him."

Julia got up and ran out, she was sobbing and I debated going after her. Cy solved the other problem; he walked across to the man and stood over him. The miner was large but flabby and Cy was ripped. His mates looked suitably embarrassed. "Shut it,

Raf," one said.

"I think," said Cy conversationally, "that you've upset the lady."

"So fucking what?" said the miner belligerently. "It needed saying. Everyone sits around here pretending that nothing's happened, that life goes on and no-one will say what they're really thinking. And your tart, the dark haired one with the bloke's name, she had a go at Clive, stuck her nose in, from what I've heard; she seems to think that it's OK." He started to rise.

Cy put his hand on the man's shoulder, his bicep bulged. The man stayed put.

"If I were you," Cy continued, "I'd stay down, and if you say that again about my friend you'll be–"

One of the women spoke up, her voice faltering with emotion, "And you miners are all so bloody perfect, aren't you? You treat us like crap until you fancy a bit, and then you wonder why we go where we get a bit of proper attention. Maybe Mike was wrong but at least he had the decency to listen to us first."

There was uproar, everyone started shouting and suddenly a plate was thrown. I spun my face, it looked like it had come from Davina, she was in amongst the women and it was headed toward Cy.

"Cy!" I shouted.

Beside me Maz was watching. "I think I'll call security," she calmly said. "You might get your day off today."

Cy had turned towards me when I shouted, still holding the miner down. The plate hit his shoulder and he flinched and stepped back. The mood changed instantly; as if it was planned the miners all rose, Cy was surrounded by them, they started throwing punches and he tried to defend himself. I saw his arms grabbed by two of the men; he was defenceless as the others started to punch his face and stomach. It was sickening. Everyone got up and moved towards the action, miners, girls. The café was turning into one of those bar-fights you see in old Westerns.

Cy was getting hurt, I wasn't having that. I grabbed the first thing

I could, the metal jug we used to froth the milk for the lattes. It was small but would have to do. Running around the counter I beat the advancing women and launched myself at the nearest of Cy's attackers. As he pulled his arm back to punch again I swung and landed the jug just below his ear. My full weight was behind it and he grunted in pain, falling to the floor. Hot milk splashed. The other three miners backed off and I stood next to Cy, who was bloodied but still very much conscious.

The women had been stunned into action by the sudden descent into violence, now they arrived in force and crowded around us, forming a barrier between the miners and Cy. I looked for Davina, she had gone. Maz was talking on the phone. Things calmed down as the alley was filled with blue flashing lights.

Chapter 23

The miners had been handcuffed and the security man watched them with suspicious eyes. The officer turned to me. "Miss... Pett," he consulted his tablet. "You're the owner of this place?"

"That's right," I said. "And I want to tell you who started it."

He looked at me. "Just the facts, Ma'am." Who did he think he was? "Now, you say there was an argument."

I sighed; it was going to be a long day. The security men had closed the café with red and black stripy tape and herded us together, customers and staff. Five uniforms were collecting statements. Cy was receiving first aid from Dr Liz. He smiled wanly, his eyes watering as his cheek was dabbed with something that clearly stung. His nose looked broken, it was blue and twice its usual cute size. And it looked like it was in the wrong place on his head.

"What happened?" the officer asked. I told him about the argument, the crying girl and Cy's attempts to calm things down. "Then a plate was thrown," I said.

"Did you see who by?" he asked me. I debated whether to say or not; was I really sure? I thought it was Davina but it could have been anyone in her group, she wasn't here anyway.

"No," I said, "there were a group over there." I waved. "And I think it came from them, it all happened so fast."

"Did the plate strike anyone?"

"Yes it hit my partner, he let go of the man he was restraining and it all kicked off."

"And the miner you assaulted, with a metal implement that you picked up, what was he doing."

Now that was going a bit far. "He was attempting to rearrange my partner's features, I decided to stop him."

"So you admit to assault, premeditated by your choice of a weapon."

"What was I supposed to use? Harsh language? Look, my partner was being held, two of these brave men were beating him, I wasn't about to stand by and let it happen. I grabbed the jug and helped even things up."

He produced handcuffs. "Very well, Miss Pett, I'm arresting you for assault."

"No you're not!"

He turned and his face registered surprise. I turned as well, although I recognised the voice. Munro was surveying the scene.

"You can't come in here," the officer said. Munro almost smiled at the naiveté.

"It's my café, officer, so technically I think you're incorrect," he replied. The officer swallowed, his eyes blinking rapidly. "And," he said surveying the scene, "it reminds me of the old days."

"I was just thinking that," shouted Dr Liz. "Memories!"

"I would be remiss if I wasn't here to look out for my tenant," Munro continued. "From what I've seen and been told, it was merely a case of handbags at ten paces. A little difference of opinions. Miss Pett was surely just protecting her employees, like any good boss should."

"Yes, Mr Munro, but she assaulted a miner with a metal milk jug, that needs to be dealt with."

Munro laughed. "A metal milk jug, it's hardly the Borgias is it?" Were they a family on the station? Or was it more history? Hang on; it had been a series on the TV, all big costumes and in the past. Why was everyone on here so obsessed with history?

"Now my friend here," he pointed at Maz, "tells me that there was a bit of shouting, started by the miners, they insulted the reputation of a lady, who left in tears. Staff attempted to sort matters out, but the more belligerent miners stirred up resentment.

A missile was thrown and things got a little heated for a while. Yes there was a little violence but really, the men are engaged on a dangerous job, it gets them wound up and it's easy to lose your temper living under such strain. No harm done, bruised egos for sure but really that's all it was." He looked at me. "Don't you agree, Miss Pett?"

What was Munro up to? Was he trying to curry favour with the miners? Or protecting Davina, or shafting Cy? Maz must have called him after she called security, what was her agenda? I was sure that there would be some motive; someone would end up owing him something which he would have pleasure in collecting. It was how people like him worked.

The officer thought about it for a moment. Munro pressed, "Think about it, all that paperwork, then your boss will have the guild on his back saying it was provocation. He won't be happy with you if all mining stops for a few days. Chandler and the station managers will get twitchy, you know how it is. Just caution everyone and let it lie."

I saw or at least I thought that I saw where this was going, Munro needed something from the miners. I had a sudden thought; maybe Davina had started it for Munro's benefit.

"It works for me, officer," I said. "There's minimal breakage and words are just that. I don't want to ban anyone, just as long as there's a promise of no repetition."

Munro gave me a 'cat's got the cream' smile. "There, Miss Pett agrees. I'm sure her partner will not want the hassle of proceedings either." I got the look again. "Will he?"

Message received. "Let me have a word, I'm sure I can make him see reason."

"You want me to do what?" Cy was incredulous. Now that his face had been cleaned up, I could see that there was a bit more damage than I had thought, he winced every time he breathed, his ribs would be bruised and painful for a few days. And he wheezed through his broken nose. But the fact that he was fit and well-muscled had saved him from a lot worse than bruising. That and my milk jug. If we were going to face this sort of thing we needed better protection than a milk jug and a ladle!

"Munro's up to something and Maz is helping him," I explained. "We're in over our heads here, let's go with the flow."

He looked at me. "And then what? We'll be Munro's stooges, we'll owe him."

"Listen, Cy, they're arresting me for assault, for all I know they'll do the same to you. The miners' union that Tina was on about, they will kick off, it'll be a major shambles. The café might be shut down and we'll have more flak than if we just suck it up."

He thought about it. "OK, but here's my demand. Once I feel better we have a couple of days off and chill. No negotiation, you were right, I need to get out of these four walls for a break, but first I'm having a lie down."

I went back to Munro and the officer. "OK," I said, "we're happy, as long as the miners understand there's no more talk about the past while they're in here. I'm not having my customers upset, any more trouble and the whole station can grind to a halt for all I care."

"There," said Munro triumphantly, "all we needed was a little common sense."

I wondered then if this would all come back to haunt me.

Chapter 24

Over the next couple of days Cy sat around while his bruises faded. He had hoped to start on deciphering the book but had been hampered by a steady stream of women bringing him succour. We had told Maz to have a few days off, she had been going non-stop and I didn't want to let her think we had taken her for granted.

They formed a disorderly queue, with plates of food, cups of coffee and in the end I let them take over the running of the café for us. Meggie came in early and cooked breakfasts and lunches. I hung around and worked the counter but I was surplus to requirements, so I used the time to get the hang of all the administration and one of the girls, actually it was Julia, helped me with the paperwork that I hadn't even realised needed doing. The accounts were all sorted; it was the hygiene and the staff that needed documenting. She was a genius with our payment terminal and showed me how it could do most of the hard work, not just the money but all the other record keeping. All I had to do was enter the details of cleaning and stock, the hours worked and it did the rest.

"Thank you for sticking up for me," I heard her say to Cy. "I heard about what happened to you after I ran out and I feel bad." He had propped himself up on cushions on one of the sofas in the corner and was overseeing operations, like a Roman Emperor surveying the slaves. There, I could do history too if I tried.

He waved her thanks away. "Don't mention it. I don't like bullies, especially men who think that because they can shout loudly they have the right to terrorise." Julia wouldn't know it, but he was speaking from experience.

"I was stupid," she admitted. "I fell for Mike, like everyone did and like everyone I thought that I would be the one who he stayed with." Her eyes misted up. "Jeff was a good man, better than I deserved, but I was told that his Scooper had a fault, that was why he hit the rock. I can't believe that he would have really killed himself."

"Cruel men say cruel things," Cy comforted her; he struggled to his feet and gave her a hug. "You don't know, and neither does that miner Raf, what really happened. If the official verdict was a mechanical fault, that should be good enough."

She sniffed. "But I'd just owned up about me and Mike, it must have affected his mind. Why were we all so stupid?"

There was no answer to that, except maybe it was human nature where emotions were concerned. Mike had caused a lot of trouble however you looked at it. But there were also people like Clarissa, who had resisted, who had been happy with what they had. So what did it say about the others, was it just the desire for a change, a bit of excitement or a fatal flaw in some females?

Mike's behaviour was wrong, but who wouldn't take what was offered. Oh God, I was getting deep in my old age. And I was missing Trevor, although I hated to admit it. I was waking up and feeling for him in the bed beside me. It must have been all the talk about what had happened in the room where I was sleeping.

A couple of days later Cy surprised me by announcing that he was off out, on his own.

"There has to be a first time," he said. "And anyway, I've been invited." He told me that Jem and Becc were taking him up to the farm to show him around, they had been telling him about it and he had found it hard to get his head around it all.

"There's a farm! OK, a window box I could believe, except that there's no windows; but a farm, with cows and ducks and fields of turnips?" I neglected to mention that it was all in the book that he *still* hadn't read. I'd sneaked a look in his room and it was on the desk where I had put it.

The girls all loved him, he made them laugh and those two were single as well, or at least uninterested and unattached, which meant that there would be no repeat of the jealous fella syndrome I had come to expect whenever men and women met up on this artificial world. He would be safe enough with them.

He had a stick, which I thought was hilarious, and he still got out of breath really quickly. He would stop and wave the stick around, or use it to point at things, nearly decapitating you if you weren't quick. They fussed around him like he was their aged relative.

Maz had come back, she saw him off with me. "It'll do him good, dear," she told me. "Get him out of here and he can relax a bit." She had returned eager to work and was surprised to find that I had also employed Davina as a cleaner. She wasn't much good at cleaning to be honest, but I felt sorry for Derek and I suppose that made me forgive the inept way she smeared the dirt around. As I wasn't sure if she had thrown the plate that had started the trouble it seemed wrong to punish her if I couldn't be certain. And it felt like something that I could do to help.

Meggie was also on the staff full-time, she did breakfasts and lunches with Cy.

I wanted to go up and see Derek again, things had stopped me. Now that we had a day free every week I could go up and get to know him a bit better.

Claire was waiting on tables and the whole operation was running smoothly. I had reorganised the baking schedule, doing it in the afternoons and evenings instead of getting up early. I had a much better idea of what I needed to make each day and timed it to coincide with the delivery. Heynrik had been replaced by a different man, was he avoiding me? Perhaps he had changed his mind and was embarrassed.

Mal, his replacement, didn't know. "I think he's just been moved over to the factory," he said. "We all get switched around, I was milking cows up to last week." Fair enough but he knew where I was, I'd be buggered if I was chasing him. I was more interested in Derek anyway; perhaps Heynrik had sensed that my interest was elsewhere.

From just wanting to escape a boring shop job and cheating bloke on Earth, I now had a café to run and, as well as Cy, five people on the payroll. It was hardly a huge concern but I was making money, the diner was still empty and Munro, at least for a while, had left me alone. Maybe I owed him a favour but he seemed to be in no hurry to collect. If I could get a date with Derek, my situation would be as near to perfect as I could hope.

I quizzed Maz about the day of the fight, was it her who had called Munro? She looked worried when I asked.

"I'm not annoyed," I said quickly. "I'm glad you did because it got me out of trouble, I just wondered why you did it."

"Violence frightens me," she said. "I saw too much of it when I was little. It made me want to be a teacher, to try and educate young people; teach them that there were other ways." Her face was animated and I knew she could see things from her past as she spoke.

"Mike, bless him, was incorrigible. He knew he was misbehaving but he couldn't help himself. And really, to start with, he did little to encourage any of them. Later when he realised the power he had, he changed."

This was priceless information, it confirmed my view on some men; give them an inch and once they've realised it's there, they'll take a lot more.

Maz continued, "From a bit of harmless fun, it turned into a contest, Mike was on a mission, he had to have as many different women as he could. Word got around about his prowess. There was almost a queue and that's when the trouble started."

"I can guess what sort of trouble you mean." I thought back to what Liz had said; beer wouldn't have helped either.

"Exactly, there were always people coming in looking for him, it got ugly, men shouting and women crying. The other customers got fed up and didn't bother coming back. It got quieter and quieter, no-one was coming in, I was thinking of quitting. Munro even came to see him, he had picked up on the disruption Mike was causing, miners were getting careless, there were accidents and women were at each other's throats. That was when Munro opened the diner."

I could imagine the mayhem; we'd had fights in the clothes shop over the last summer dress, bribes and threats. And that was just over a few frocks.

"Munro has a bad reputation," she said. "Sure he's a ruthless businessman, but he cares about the station and the smooth running of things. Mike told Munro it was none of his business how he lived. Munro disagreed, said that the station was in danger."

That seemed a little dramatic. "Surely not?"

"It was," Maz nodded. "The station's like a spider's web, it looks so solid; so big and strong but it's really weak. If there's trouble amongst the miners, the mining slows down. If the farmers get pissed off, the crops don't grow. If there's anything that might cause a drop in profits the company panics. All it takes is a little thing and suddenly it's out of balance."

I remembered what Derek had said, *this place is an eco-system, like Earth.* As we had seen there, it was the little things that caused the big problems. I might not know my history but I knew enough about Earth's recent past. A bit of plastic in the sea, carbon emissions, unfair politics, there were so many to choose from. The law of unintended consequences. OK, Earth was much larger but all that meant was that this place would need a lot less of a nudge to descend into chaos.

"Mike told Munro to get stuffed, said it was his life and he'd do what he pleased. Munro was annoyed and warned him to behave. Mike just laughed in his face. On his way out Munro took me to one side. He said that he could see that I was upset and if I ever had a problem in the café I was to call him, he would come in and protect me. When it all started again I just did it automatically."

That was interesting; it showed me a new side to Munro, was it just the caring side of a megalomaniac? Or was he really someone who cared about the station? But even though it showed that Mike and Munro were not the best of friends, was it enough to make him a murderer?

Chapter 25

Cy returned from his trip and he was buzzing. "You've seen the farm," he said, his eyes shining. "You never said how brilliant it was."

"I only saw the wheat fields," I answered. "I didn't think that it would be your thing."

"Neither did I, but after all the desolation of Mars and the steel walls in here, it was like being back on Earth. Some bloke was telling me, because they can control the conditions so well, they can go from seed to harvest in three months, every crop, every time. They have tractors and harvesters, all the labour saving gear."

"What do those girls do up there?"

"They work in the processing plant, the crops and animals are… well, processed. They thresh and grind grain, butcher meat, make sausages, collect eggs and bag it all up. And there's an automated bakery. They do cheese and make ready meals for the miners while they're out working; it's a huge operation. I don't know what doesn't go on up there food and drink-wise. It's all organic as well. And it's not just a few people; there are loads of them working up there. One said that there were more farmers than miners. Considering the level of automation that they have, there's far more than they need. But it's just like a big family, Derek, the boss—"

"I've met him," I butted in. "He's Davina's father."

He nodded. "I know, don't interrupt, he mentioned you, and it was more than just a mention, he wanted to know all about you, were you single? All sorts of stuff. I bigged you up, I think he fancies you. You can thank me later."

Great, Cy playing ham-fisted Cupid; that was all I needed. I liked

Derek, he was older than I was, not that that bothered me, more important was that Davina worked in the café; it might be an issue if she thought I was moving in, replacing her mother in Derek's affections.

"Where was I?" he said. "There are some really friendly people up there too. They didn't know we were open again, I've told them all to come down when they have a chance, they have their own canteen but they reckon it's crap. I had a meal and it's not but then, they're in there every day, and…" Cy was buzzing, clearly he had found kindred spirits. "There's a card school most nights, and… they brew their own hooch!"

I didn't know about the organic thing but I'd thought there was something about the food, it tasted so different to the mass produced, additive filled stuff you ate on Earth, or even on Mars come to that. And a card game, that was Cy's weakness, he used to play cards in London. He would lose a fortune, win it back and lose it again.

"There's a park as well, did you know? We should get up there; stuck in here all day's not right."

I felt like saying, if you'd read the book that I'd given you ages ago, then you'd know but I bit my tongue. Cy was one of those who had to see it for themselves, then complain that you hadn't told them.

What he said about Derek interested me as well. I knew why he was single; perhaps I shouldn't worry about Davina's feelings, she was an adult after all, maybe I ought to go up and introduce myself properly. But if he was so interested, why hadn't he come to see me?

Chapter 26

Tina came in. "Come down tomorrow, at about ten," she said, as she grabbed a coffee to go, "I've got us time on the simulator and if you're OK we can go out for real one day next week."

Cy was itching to go and explore again. His interest had been aroused by what the ladies had told him and his trip to the farm. He told me that in a way, he was glad that there had been the fight; it had made him shake himself and want to get out. Now he wanted to go to the gym, picnic in the park and go to the cinema amongst other things. The cinema; Heynrik had said he would take me, he still hadn't been in touch, he must have lost interest. I didn't care, I had enough to keep me busy.

"We'll go to the park soon, Cy," I promised him. "Tina's taking me on the simulator tomorrow, how do you fancy a go?"

He shuddered. "No way, thanks all the same. I'll stick to the farm in space, it's a lot more sensible."

"It's a simulator, Cy. We won't be going anywhere, it'll only be like watching it on TV. Or playing a video game." Then I remembered how that affected him.

Next day, I went down to the hangar deck and found my way to Tina's bench. She was hitting something very hard with a big hammer. I hung around; I didn't want to distract her in case she clobbered herself. She eventually saw me and stopped. "Hi," she said. "Are you ready?"

"Don't let me disturb your hitting things."

"It's all part of my therapy." She grinned. "I pretend it's a bloke."

"Anyone in particular?" It was pretty obvious that, whoever it was, they had made a deep and lasting impression.

She hesitated, just for a second. "No, in my experience they're all the same."

That sounded sad to me, she might not have been as naturally attractive as Lou or Terri but she didn't deserve to feel like that. Maybe the welder persona put them off. Or the shaved head.

"Tina, I hope you don't mind me asking, but why do you shave your head?"

She shrugged. "It's no big deal, I sometimes have to spacewalk, repair things outside." That sounded like a big deal to me, I hoped she wasn't setting me up for a spacewalk.

"The hair used to get squashed in the suit; it would itch when I took the helmet off. One of the old hands said it was more comfortable to shave it off. I tried it and it was. Then I got into the habit, it was a lot easier than constantly washing it and conditioning it and all the agonising over whether it looked nice."

That was logical, and sort of liberating.

"Right then, let's get you into the simulator," she said. She led me around the workshops to a small lift. "This is the secure lift," she explained. "I expect you went in it when you went up to the observatory."

I nodded. "Yeah, Terri took me, it's amazing up there."

"Not half as amazing as cruising up to it from the outside and looking in," she said. "This lift's the only way of getting where we're going, except for the platform we use to get the Scoopers up to the workshop."

We went down a deck to the actual hangars. There were lines of all of the craft that I had seen in the workshop. And there were so many more of them.

Tina explained them to me as we walked past each row. "The big one is the spare shuttle; it has the range to get to Mars, big engines and room for a dozen or so, plus all the food and stuff you'd need. Then there're the mining craft, they're all based around the same design, just with different bits welded on the front, depending on what job they're doing. Half of them are out, we can just squeeze them all in if we have to but normally the next shift will take this lot out before the others come back in."

All the craft were painted yellow, some had what looked like train buffers mounted on hydraulic arms and others had cranes or baskets on them. Each had two big rubber pipes attached to them just behind the cabs. "The big pipe is fuel, the small one is oxygen in and carbon dioxide out. That's where the farm comes in; the growing plants in the farm absorb the carbon dioxide and produce oxygen, so we need the farm to keep mining. Of course they need the miners as well, part of every rock is ice, the water goes to irrigate the fields, amongst other things."

I suddenly saw the interdependence of the two parts of the station; Maz was right, it was like a spider's web.

"What about the fuel? Where does that come from?"

Tina grinned. "There's a lot of methane produced on the station, by farm animals, rotting waste, us. It's all turned into fuel for the station in the core, how they do it is well beyond me but the same fuel that powers the station is used to power these."

At the end of the rows of each type there was one sat on its own. It looked just like the rest, except for the cables coming from underneath it, leading away in an underfloor conduit.

"Every type has the same simulator, they're all the same to drive," Tina explained. "You can tell the simm by the cables underneath, and they're always parked on the left-hand end of the line."

We climbed into the cabin of the craft, it was fitted with a basket; it was quite a tight fit for two of us. There were two seats, one behind the other and not much else. Did someone really spend twelve hours in here, mining or scooping or whatever it was called? I felt claustrophobic after less than a minute. "There's normally only one seat in the mining craft," Tina explained. "Only the sim and the one used for practical testing and examinations have two fixed in, although you can add a second to any of them." She pulled the hatch shut and locked it.

I sat in the front seat. There was a console with a few gauges and switches, my hands rested on a steering wheel on a stalk, just like a car would have. A lever by my left hand was probably a control for the basket arrangement that was mounted on the front; I expected that I would find out soon enough. There was a single pedal and my right foot rested on it naturally. The windows looked normal, I had expected them to be different in a simulator, maybe with some sort of projector over them. I asked Tina how it worked.

"There's a projecting layer built into the glass, it only comes on when you start the engine. This is an old decommissioned Scooper, it's not airtight, but otherwise identical."

She leant over and pointed at a row of digital counters, they read oxygen, fuel and load. Oxygen and fuel were at one hundred per cent, load was zero. "Listen carefully," said Tina. "If you ever go out for real, keep your eyes on the fuel and oxygen numbers. They'll go down quickly once you start working; an alarm will sound at twenty per cent. If you hear that, get back to the station straight away, don't forget."

She flipped a red switch on the console and there was a rumble behind me as the engines started up. The Scooper vibrated slightly, adding to the realism. The view outside didn't change.

"I thought that you said the screens came on when you started up the engine?"

Tina sighed and I realised that I'd done it again. "We haven't MOVED yet," she said, exasperated. "Why would the picture change?"

"I thought that we would start off outside," I said. "I expected to see stars or something."

"What and miss the best bit, this is a total simulation, you do the whole thing here." She leant over past me and pushed the button marked 'Radio'.

"Hello, Control," she said. "This is Scooper 1; we're just going for a spin."

"What are you doing?"

"It's voice activated, the whole system's automatic, no human input. Everything you say and do from now on is recorded; it's good for analysing what you did; or didn't. It's important procedure anyway, you always tell someone when you're going out with a real one, and this gets you into the habit. And simulators are always number 1, so Scooper 1 or Shuttle 1 or whatever 1."

"So is anyone listening to us now?"

She shrugged her shoulders. "There's no way to tell. You can turn it off if you want privacy." She pointed to the button. "It shows in the mining control room when the sim is in use, if they're bored they might put it on the screen and watch, see how you do."

I'd better try and behave then, I needed to take this seriously but still didn't really see how it could be realistic. I knew I was in a stationary broken old Scooper secured to the hangar deck. The view was boring.

"The wheel turns you," she said. "Pull it towards you to go up, push it away to go down, the pedal controls speed. There's no brake as such, it's all automatic, as you ease the pedal some of the thrust is reversed to slow you down." I thought that the controls were a bit simple, how hard could it be to drive one of these?

"If you're ready, pull the wheel toward you," she said. I did and I was immediately jolted out of my skin, it felt like the Scooper thing lifted up. The view out of the port changed. Startled, I let go and we dropped back to the deck with a bump.

"Realistic isn't it?" she said. "We're mounted on a hydraulic platform. Now open the hatch and do that again."

I did and I could see the difference immediately, looking out of the open hatch I could see that we were still on the deck, looking through the Scooper's ports I could see that the view was different; it didn't line up with the view through the hatch. It looked like we had moved, but we hadn't. With the vibration and the change of view it had fooled me. It was eerie; I could have sworn that I had felt motion. I felt cheated, like I had been conned somehow.

I shut the hatch again. "Now press the pedal." I did, gently, and the wall got closer as we moved forward, or at least the picture said that we were moving forward. I *knew* we weren't but it didn't seem to matter to my brain.

"Drive into the lock," she said, she leant across and flipped a switch on the panel in front of me. I saw the wall move sideways as a door opened.

And so it went on, the door shut behind us, I could see it in the mirror. It was just like being there. I landed on the deck, again there was the bump. Tina flipped more switches. "You should be doing this."

"OK, tell me which one to press." I looked and the switches were all labelled.

"Now we have to wait for the air to be sucked out and we can open the door," she said, pointing. There was a read-out by the outer door, the big red numbers on it reduced as the oxygen was emptied out of the airlock. I started to concentrate on my breathing. Bloody hell, I was buying into the illusion, trouble was, it was just so convincing.

"You can't help it can you?" said Tina, and she was right; it was frighteningly realistic. "Make sure your straps are nice and tight," she advised. I wondered why, we were stationary.

The door opened. "Away we go then." I pushed the pedal as she reported to Control.

I felt my stomach swoop as the station fell astern; there was nothing ahead of us at all, just blackness with the twinkling of a few million stars. I looked down and saw that the floor was transparent, and there was nothing below us; nothing. My stomach started performing acrobatics.

"Push down on the wheel," said Tina and I nearly barfed as the view tilted and the nothing below us became the nothing in front of us. I felt like I was travelling down, with no bottom in sight. It felt like I was falling out of the chair, now I saw the reason for the straps.

In a panic I pulled up on the wheel and the view shifted rapidly, there was nothing above me either. "Oh God! I'm going to be sick," I shouted.

Tina was laughing. "Turn the wheel," she suggested and the planet swung past us. "Right; now open the hatch again."

What? For a moment I hesitated, wouldn't we die? Then I shook my head. I opened the hatch. My brain felt like it would explode, I could see how my senses had been fooled by a rumble and the clever projection onto the windows. I looked back, the stars shone on the screen.

"Get back in here," said Tina and I did, shutting the hatch.

"Now," she said, "first of all, if we were out for real you couldn't forget and open the hatch, it's locked when the engine starts. And you wouldn't want to do it anyhow. Now you know that it's safe, just have a play."

I took the controls again and did just that. It was really exciting driving around and I soon found myself in amongst the rocks of the ring system. From a distance it had all looked so sedate, close up it was like billiards on a moving table, rocks were coming at me from all directions and every time one got close an alarm would sound.

"If the machine reckons it hit you then you failed, but as you're not training we won't worry too much about it." I wanted to do it right though and after a while I found that I was looking all around me automatically and dodging the rocks. The alarm sounded less and less as time went on but it was exhausting.

"Do the miners really do this for twelve hours at a stretch?"

"Yes they do, they have a short break every hour or so but they're out here for twelve."

I'd got the hang of looking around and dodging the rocks, the Scooper was really responsive to the controls, I had thought them to be pretty basic but they actually enabled you to drive without thinking. After a fair while had passed, Tina suggested that I try and return to the station.

I had a sudden panic, where was I? With all the flying about I had completely lost track of where the station was. Never mind, it was huge; I'd soon spot it.

Of course I couldn't find it; I got worried and turned the Scooper all ways, nope. Space was black and starry all around me. I was lost. And I'd been doing so well. I felt devastated, and then I could hear Tina, who had been quiet since she suggested it, sniggering quietly to herself. "And what's so bloody funny?" I asked.

"They all do it," she said, between giggles. "They all go charging around then suddenly realise that they're lost. They think, that's OK, the station is huge, it's got lights on, but they can't find it."

So it wasn't just me. "What do I do then?" I said, feeling slightly better to know that I wasn't the only dozy bird who couldn't find the biggest man-made structure in the universe. Tina didn't seem concerned; mind you she knew that we were still in the hangar. But this was supposed to be an accurate simulation; there must be an answer.

"Well, the people who designed the Scoopers thought of it, so they put that there. She leant over and pointed to a small green button. Above it, it said 'Auto-Return'.

"That's a built-in navigation computer, it only does one thing, it homes you into the station and the airlock you came out of."

I pressed the button and the Scooper took over, I could feel it pull at the controls and I let go. The Scooper turned and accelerated towards a patch of stars that looked no different to any other but as we went along I saw a shadow, which grew bigger as we approached it. Soon I could make out flashing lights and all the comforts of home. I felt us slow down and saw the airlock door open. The Scooper altered course slightly and in no time at all we were inside.

I was a bit sad when Tina told me to turn the engine off, I'd enjoyed myself a lot more than I could have imagined, and for most of the time I had forgotten that I was in a simulator.

"You're pretty good," Tina said as we climbed out of the seats. "I reckon you could make a fair go of the real thing." That was praise indeed and if someone had offered me a job scooping right then, I would have gone for it.

"Thanks for that," I said as I stood by the Scooper, my legs were a bit wobbly and Tina grinned as I held on to it for balance. "I haven't enjoyed myself so much for ages," I said. "I don't want to leave it all behind."

"What do you reckon then, Andi, do you fancy a real trip?"

I did, what a turn up. "I reckon I do," I said.

Tina walked with me back to her office, just by the lift.

"I don't weld all the time," she explained. "I'm a trainer for the new miners and I'm one of the examiners as well. I do the practical exam with them before they're allowed to fly solo; we go out for real and catch some rocks. If you're serious about learning we can make it official, get you trained."

She gave me a thick pack of papers in a fancy folder. "Have a read and fill the forms in," she suggested. "We can have you trained and certified to fly in no time."

"Isn't it a lot of work?"

Her reply surprised me. "No, what you've done now will be logged, you only need four hours and an exam pass for your reserve list ticket, another ten hours real life playing with the rocks for a full Scooper licence."

I was feeling great as Tina took me back in the small lift to the café. "Oh, and if you pass the exam you get a key-card for the small lift," she told me. Better and better, I could go up to the observatory.

When I got back to the café, Cy was in full smirk mode. "Oh God! I'm going to be sick," he said, imitating my voice. "Your face was a picture."

I rounded on him; I was angry and confused at the same time. "How did you know?" Surely Tina hadn't had time to tell him while I was coming back, then I remembered, she had said that you could go up to the control room and see it on their monitors.

"Did you go up and watch?"

He nodded. "Lou came in just after you left, her ankle is OK now and she wanted to catch up. I told her where you had gone and she took me up, or was it down, I can't remember, anyway we went and had a look."

"What did you think?"

"It's convincing, isn't it? They had all sorts of camera angles and full voice recording. The duty officer said they love watching people's faces; they call the simulator the vomit comet."

"Are you game for a go then? I'm going to train properly. I've got the papers and everything!"

"No," he said. "I've made my mind up to stick to what I know, and that's not out there."

Chapter 27

We were going to have our day out together; Cy had healed some more, he showed me the bruises, they were multicoloured but fading fast. He said that he felt fit enough for a brisk walk. He had been enjoying all the attention but he wanted to explore.

"Let's go to the park, we could take a picnic and just chill."

"Good plan, but first we have to sort the electrician out, he still hasn't been."

So we packed up some of Clarissa's pies and a couple of bottles of water. I stashed the book at the bottom of my bag as well, for safekeeping while we left the café unattended. We were closed anyway, this was our day off. The ladies said that they would open up but I wanted to have one day a week where we didn't do anything.

Cy had not been to the admin offices, he saw the queue and his face fell. "I'll go for a stroll," he said as I stood in line.

This time the wait was shorter and when I got to the front, there was a different person to my last visit.

"What can we do for you?" she asked, after I had identified myself.

"I need to know when the electrician I asked for will be coming."

She hunted through her screens. "I can't find any record of a request," she said.

Typical. "About a week ago, I gave the lady a list and she scanned it. The stores I asked for have arrived and the garbage has gone but there's been no electrician."

She went through the screens again. "No, hang on. I've got your list here and it does say electrician. I'll put in a new request, they should be along tomorrow."

Bureaucracy, oh well at least it was in progress, and we wouldn't miss our day out waiting for them.

I left the office and found Cy; he was standing outside a place that advertised equipment hire, he looked pleased.

"I've rented us a scanner; they'll bring it around tomorrow, now we can copy the book."

"Well done, Cy. I'm finished. The electrician will be along tomorrow as well, let's hit the park."

We took the lift up to the park level and exited on a new world.

After the obligatory disinfectant, we were faced with a brightly lit expanse of short cropped grass that was dotted with fruit trees and wooden benches. The smell of fresh-cut grass lingered in the air and a gentle breeze rustled leaves. There were small groups of people sitting, walking or just lazing around. Over in the distance a game of football seemed to be in progress. The place was lit by diffuse light, and looking up there was the appearance of cloud cover. There was no external clue, no picture windows, if you had been brought here asleep and awoken, you would have thought you were back on Earth, in a park on a warm but overcast day.

"Not at all what I expected," Cy remarked as we strolled across the grass, it felt fantastic after the hard steel decks and I kicked off my shoes, in my mind I was back in London, strolling on Blackheath, glimpsing the river through the buildings on a hazy day. And there was a river, well a big stream actually, it looked so natural meandering across the space, bridged here and there with wooden arches. The water ran over rocks with a soothing sound, it must have been pumped, the deck was level after all but it looked so natural, dragonflies darted. Derek had done an amazing job.

Cy was out of breath, I could tell that his ribs must still be hurting. "Let's sit here by the water, Cy," I suggested and I think he was relieved to plonk himself down. I wanted to have a day free from books and burglars and dead lotharios. But first I had to know Cy's plan.

"What are we going to do with the book?" He looked around, we were alone.

"Once I've copied it, I can scrawl notes on the pages as I try and work it out."

"You got any ideas?"

"Sure, like I said before, I reckon it's a substitution code, simple once you know where he's started."

"What's a substitution code when it's at home then?"

He rolled his eyes, as if everyone knew what a substitution code was.

"Just what it says, it's a really simple basic code, you just substitute letters, you use another letter instead of the real one." Hooray! He was explaining in words of one syllable.

"Oh right, and as long as you know which one means what then you can decode it."

"That's right, it's easy, after a while you can probably do it without notes. With a bit of luck he's just started the alphabet in a different place, so maybe every A is a C, then B is a D, C is an E, and so on. You can see which letter is used most, that will be E, that gives you a clue."

That sounded easy enough. "And if not?"

"Ah, that's where it gets more complicated, he might have jumbled the letters up so they're not in order. And there's numbers in there too, but no spaces. At its simplest, it's enough to stop the casual look, but it can be incredibly complicated. It all depends how secure he wanted it to be. Each page might be in a different code, although I doubt that. I don't suppose it was ever meant to be found. More like an insurance policy or just personal like a diary."

The thought of its existence would be enough to stop most dissent; I expect he got the idea from Munro.

"Right, Cy, that's enough of that, let's just chill and enjoy being away from it all for a day."

We sat and watched the world go by; or at least the artificially pumped water in the fake stream on the space station.

"Derek says this place is just like Earth only on a smaller scale," I said. "I must go and see him again."

"You'd be silly not to, he must wonder why you haven't, especially now that Davina is working for you; that should get you some points."

"That wasn't the idea, Cy, but maybe you're right." My mind drifted away; I was sitting here with Derek, he had his arm around my waist and I was leaning into him. It felt nice.

Cy nudged me. "Wake up, Andi, we have company."

I came back to reality and saw Heynrik, he had spotted me and was coming our way. "Hi, Andi, Cy, how are you both?" He sat between us. "I've missed you, I got taken off deliveries and I've been working on the farm. My boss got me helping out in the factory."

"I thought you were avoiding me." Did that sound desperate?

He laughed. "Now why would I do that, I'm asking you out, remember?"

I hadn't forgotten, but where would he take me? Cy got to his feet. "I'll leave you two to it," he said, and he hobbled off.

"What happened to him?" Heynrik asked and I had to tell him about the fight in the café.

"Oh dear," he looked shocked. "I'm not surprised though, the café has bad memories for a lot of people." I wondered if he would mention Morgana, I decided not to, it would hardly be tactful, not that I was renowned for my tact.

"How about coming with me to the cinema?" he asked. "There's little point in taking you for a candlelit meal in the diner is there?"

That was true, I hadn't thought about evening meals, maybe we could branch out, thanks to the non-appearance of the electrician we had the soft lighting.

"Sounds fine to me," I said. "What sort of films do they show?"

"Who knows, whatever arrives on the shuttle."

I knew from the book that there was little else to do, if you weren't a gym bunny or working there was little leisure activity. There was a library and I guess the park never got dark, or perhaps it did. But Cy had also mentioned card games and illegal booze, maybe there were other hidden worlds within this world. The cinema was probably a good, safe place to start.

"Sure, pick me up anytime." There, I was sounding desperate again. Would he notice?

He smiled. "And how about the day after tomorrow, say half past six? We can go up to the observation platform first, I'll call for you."

"It sounds perfect, what do you observe?"

"Wait and see," he said, he got up and walked off.

"So you have a date." Cy must have been watching, and listening. As soon as Heynrik left he was straight back and he sat down with a sigh. "Lucky you, don't do anything I wouldn't."

On Earth I would have said, 'That leaves me plenty to get up to then,' but now it didn't feel like the right sort of comment, perhaps it was the knowledge of Heynrik and Morgana and Mike's intervention. Not to mention Lou. Maz was right, it was a goldfish bowl, everyone was connected.

We ate our picnic, people walked past and said hello, the football game ebbed and flowed, near us then far away.

Cy looked longingly at it. "Perhaps I could join in when my bloody ribs don't hurt," he muttered.

"I'm sure they'd let you, does that mean you're getting integrated?"

"Yes I think I am, I like it here, the people I've met have been friendly and nobody's judged me. I've changed my opinion; you've changed as well; this place has had an effect on you."

"What do you mean?"

"You're getting so much more serious than you used to be, what happened to the crazy lady?"

I hadn't noticed but maybe I was, I had certainly learned a lot since I had found Trevor and Maisie in my bed, my dreams of happily ever after had been shattered and there was no going back.

The more I found out about Mike the more cynical I was becoming; maybe I was thinking, if men can do it, why not women?

"I don't know, Cy; maybe I just grew up and woke up."

When we got back to the café, there was a note jammed into the shutters, the electrician had called, it said that he would be back later. The alleyway lights had been fixed though, which was a start.

Chapter 28

I read through the paperwork that Tina had given me, a whole lot of rules and procedures for driving Scoopers and the myriad other types of craft that the miners operated. It seemed that I could get qualified to drive one very easily, a fact that amazed me. All I had to do was complete a practical test and fill in a few forms. The practical test would have a few questions thrown in on radio work and safety. I filled the forms out and deposited them in the admin centre. And then I forgot all about it.

It had been a busy day, I was shattered. Heynrik was calling for me in an hour. I wondered if I was only going out with him because he had asked; I'd really have preferred to have gone out with Derek. But despite my growing cynicism, I hadn't done anything about what I really wanted, just gone with the flow, tried to make sure that everyone else was happy.

Cy said that I had changed but had I? Looking back, maybe I had only gone out with Trevor for the same reason.

Tonight, I decided, was just a first date. Heynrik was nice but it wouldn't go further, there would be no second. I really wanted Derek. I was going to get what I wanted this time, not just go along with things to keep the peace.

The portable scanner had arrived. Cy took it into the back and copied the book onto a memory card and printed out a set of pages as well. No electrician had turned up; again.

Somehow the word of my impending date had got around. Claire and Meggie had known when they arrived. "You'll love the observation platform," Meggie said. "It has this effect on people and... well, you'll love it."

Claire nodded. "It's amazing, in more ways than one," she added in a dreamy voice.

Terri came in with a load of cakes the twins had made mid-morning, she was full of it. "I hear you and Heynrik are off to the observation platform tonight," she said, "and then on to the cinema."

"I was meaning to tell you, it sort of got sprung on me. I hope it's not treading on Lou's toes."

She shook her head. "No, that's over, not that it was ever really a big thing, they had a few dates but I think that it was more of a rebound, at least for him."

"The one thing I've realised," I said, "is that because of the small population, everyone on here is connected, whether you like it or not."

"That's so true," she agreed. "Sometimes I think you shouldn't say or do anything because of the effect it has on everything else."

Since our little conversation in the stairwell, Terri had seemed more thoughtful. Maybe she was worried that, despite what I had said, I would spill the beans on her if I ever found the book. Or that someone else would get hold of it. Now that we had found it, I wondered if she somehow knew, I had tried not to change my behaviour but I was notoriously bad at hiding secrets. "See you later, have a good evening," she said as she left.

The rest of the day was the usual mix of rush and quiet, Davina came in after lunch, she had gone back to working mornings at her admin job, she only teased our bacteria part-time. I didn't let her in the kitchen, that needed cleaning properly, but she was improving and even though she could be a surly teenager I didn't mind her. She told me that Derek liked the shortbread I made and asked if she could be paid a box a week instead of money, so he could have them.

I thought that was really sweet of her and let her have them for nothing. She was never surly when talking about Derek, she loved him to bits and the fact that she had stayed with him showed it.

She never mentioned her mother. I considered telling her about my plan to get Derek to ask me out, and then I thought better of it. It might not be the best thing to tell her I had designs on her father, especially as she almost certainly knew all about my impending date. I hoped she would be gone before Heynrik arrived.

It was just after five and we were closing up, I had hoped that I would be left in peace to get ready but everyone seemed to be hanging around. Cy had come out of his room for a snack, I guess he had been working on the book all day; apart from coffee and lunch I hadn't seen him.

"That was our busiest day yet." Maz punched buttons on the terminal. "Look how much we're making."

The number was a lot larger than last time, the system was so clever that it deducted wages and invoices in real time, so the number on the screen was always our profit and for the first time it showed that we had enough to buy return tickets to Earth if we wanted.

Not that I did, but it represented freedom, and it felt good.

"Hey, Cy, have you seen the figures?"

He looked up; he was actually reading the guidebook, eating toast. "What, are we in profit?"

"Not just profit, we can afford to go back to Earth for a break if we want."

"You know, not long ago I would have bitten your arm off for that, but now, I don't really care."

I felt the same, I was enjoying myself, the work had settled into a routine and now I had a date. Thoughts of Mike and books could wait.

"Right, I'm off for a shower," I said, Maz looked quizzical, she was about to start cleaning things and I normally helped her. "What about finishing up here?"

"Cy's doing that."

"She's got a date!" he shouted.

"Oh yes, of course she has, that's exciting, dear." Maz had a twinkle in her eye; I remembered that there was no Mr Maz. "You carry on then, tell me again, who's the lucky guy?"

"It's Heynrik," Cy announced and her face fell, she quickly recovered but I had seen the look. "You have a wonderful time," she said, turning to the coffee machine and attacking it with her cloth.

As I showered I wondered what the look had been for, maybe Maz had a crush on Heynrik, she was single after all, she might have been old but that meant little, she still looked stunning, acted young and was fun to be with. And why was she pretending that she didn't know? She had been there when Claire and I were talking about it this morning. She didn't forget things, ever. Who knows, I thought as I gave the bedroom a quick tidy, this was a first date but it never hurt to be prepared.

I showered and dressed, not in the boiler suit this time but in a real dress and courts. It felt weird to be bare legged. I left my hair down after I had straightened it; it had grown a lot and hung to mid-back.

Looking in the mirror I applied just a touch of make-up, again it felt weird, I was out of practise at this dating thing, how should I behave? I had known Heynrik for a while but didn't really know him at all. He seemed to know Lou but she had never said that they were an item; at least I had checked with Terri first.

I went back through the café. "You scrub up OK," Cy told me. "I'd forgotten about women's legs with all the boiler suits on here."

"You don't think it's too much?"

"It looks very nice, dear," Maz joined in. "What do you think, Claire?" Oh no it was a fashion show, I had made the dress myself and was quite proud of it but the few I had seen on the station were just as nice, at least in my eyes. Claire came over, so did Davina, pausing in her grease distribution duties to come and have a look.

"Lovely," was Claire's opinion, but she didn't sound like she was over the moon. Davina burst into tears and ran into the kitchen. Oh God, what had I done now?

"I'll go," Maz said as I just stood there, feeling very self-conscious. I wanted to put the boiler suit back on.

Claire filled me in. "It was a shock to us both. In that dress you looked just like Davina's mother."

I was saved from any more comparison by Heynrik, simply dressed in jeans and a shirt, at least he didn't look like anyone's father, or if he did it wasn't mentioned.

"Hello, Andi," said Heynrik. "You're looking nice, shall we go?" How long had he been there? He took my arm and led me away from the café.

We rode in the lift, it stopped at each accommodation deck and more people entered. They were all dressed for an evening out and my outfit was no different to most of the ladies that I saw. Everyone smiled and a few of the men did a double-take, apart from the day we arrived I had worn jeans or a boiler suit and I must have looked completely different.

We got off the lift at level four, as did just about everyone else. I vaguely remembered from the guide that the first four levels were farming and wondered what we were doing here.

I found out as we all exited. We walked past the airlock and entered a wide doorway up a few steps. We emerged onto a platform, suspended over a large field. The outer walls of the station on this deck were transparent and the majesty of the universe could be seen, Saturn dominated but there were at least a million other things to see. At the inner edge of the platform, a rail prevented us from falling into a rural scene that could have graced a chocolate box. Cows grazed below us, on bright green grass and in the middle distance a row of what looked like apple trees formed a natural barrier to more livestock. It was so out of place, compared to the view in the other direction.

Heynrik put his arm around my waist, I revelled in the contact, he smelt like the seaside when we used to go on holiday, after Cy's toilet cleaner aroma it was like going back in time. It was better than my daydreaming in the park. We strolled along the walkway, as did all the other people, and chatted.

"I used to come up here all the time," he told me. "It was such a contrast; somehow it put things into perspective."

"It's glorious," I said, I didn't really know what to say, did he mean with Morgana or at some other time?

"My last girlfriend, Morgana, hated it here, after we split up and she went back to Mars, I used to come here alone and think a lot."

That was a relief; he had got it out in the open. "And I ought to tell you," he added. "I have dated Lou, but nothing serious, she tried to cheer me up after Morgana left and I appreciated it, but we were never more than friends."

I had not expected him to say that, I stopped and took him in my arms. "Thank you for your honesty," I said as we kissed. I was pleased to find that he was a good kisser. So much for my resolve to make this a platonic first and last date.

We sat on one of the benches, closely entwined and oblivious to the passing couples, snogging like two teenagers. When I came up for air I couldn't help noticing that most of the other people were engaged in the same activity, standing or sitting. Some were even lying down on the deck!

"It's the place," Heynrik whispered. "It seems to bring out the romantic in everyone."

That was what Meggie and Claire had meant; it seemed a bit public to me but I bent my head back in towards him. "It does," I said as we started kissing again.

We missed the film, sitting and snogging, then watching the cosmos, then watching the farm, then snogging again. I felt like a teenager and loved it. When Heynrik suggested we go somewhere a bit quieter I was more than ready. That was me all over; I could never keep to a plan.

Cy had already told me that he would be gone when I got back; he was off playing cards and drinking unofficial home brew, the one that Jem and Becc had been on about. It was made from potato peelings smuggled out of the processing plant. Cy had brought a few bottles back to the café and stashed them in the lounge. It was like paint stripper but OK with orange juice. He leered when he told me I would have the place to myself. "I won't be back till the morning; you can make as much noise as you want!"

Heynrik and I sat in the lounge, alternately sipping the home brew and kissing. Cy would never notice that one bottle had gone. The alcohol was going to my head but I was relaxed and things were progressing nicely towards the inevitable. It had been a long while for me and I was just about ready.

"I'm just going to the bathroom," I said. "Give me a couple of minutes and follow me."

I walked slightly unsteadily down to my bedroom and into the bathroom. I sat down and realised that there was no paper. Bugger! I looked around, the spare rolls were in the stores, it wouldn't be very romantic to ask Heynrik to fetch me some, the moment would be lost. And I didn't want that.

Then I remembered the wad of tissue that I had pushed into the hole in the wall, it would have to do. I pulled it out and heard a scraping noise. Peering through the hole I saw that Heynrik was in Cy's bedroom, searching in Cy's drawers. I sobered up really fast as I crept out of the bathroom and along the alley towards the door.

Chapter 29

"Looking for something?"

Heynrik dropped the drawer frame and turned, his face a mixture of shock and guilt.

"I suppose a leg-over's out of the question now?" My God, he was hoping to shag his way out of this!

"Too right, buster." If I said that I was annoyed, that would be putting it mildly. I was feeling frustrated and I was very annoyed. Heynrik moved towards me, saw my face and thought better of it. He just stood there; I had to break the silence.

"Was it all a lie then, were you just trying to get into my pants to get in here and search the place?"

"No, Andi," he said. "Well, yes at first it might have been but then no. I really like you, Andi." He wasn't really convincing me there.

He moved towards me again. "I wouldn't," I warned him. "I'm not in a forgiving mood at the moment."

"It's not what you think," he tried again. He was still on the wrong tack.

"It never is, is it to do with Morgana?"

He swallowed. "How do you... never mind, I guess everyone knows. I was OK until I saw you tonight, it just reminded me, seeing you; you reminded me of her, and then, when we ended up in here, I'm not used to drinking, it seemed like an idea. I'd only be a minute." His shoulders slumped and he sat on the bed.

I sat in the armchair; it was a safe distance from him, safe for him that was. "Get talking then."

He looked like he was about to cry, not that that would get him any points, the words came out like a river, unstoppable.

"Morgana was a lot like you, feisty and independent, we were happy together until Mike moved in on her. Like a lot of the women on here, she fell for him and I'm sure he messed with her head. It was all a game to him; he had some sort of psychological way of talking to them, like you see on the videos. I always thought it was a fake, I mean, how could you make people do things? But he could. He made them, her, dependant on him, then he would dump them for the next adventure. But the others he dumped, he seemed to leave them feeling OK, they never hated him, just accepted it and moved on. But not her. Somehow I think he must have convinced her that if I found out I would hurt her."

Heynrik obviously had no idea about females and the way they thought, poor bloke. Some were tough, they could take it and move on, others were broken up, it was called emotion. If I'd felt less desire to beat him around the head I might have tried to explain.

"Hold on, what do you mean found out?" This was important. "Found out what?"

"I'm coming to that. I think the worry of it made her leave the station. But I didn't know anything about it at the time. She just disappeared. One day I came back to the apartment and she wasn't there. I didn't know where she had gone. I checked everywhere; sure she was on the station. In the end I had to ask departures and that's when I found that she had left." He stopped for a second. "I have to go to the toilet."

"OK but you're not running away." I went with him and stood outside, I could hear him being sick. It must have been the home brew and getting caught.

He came out. "Sorry," he said. "That stuff's strong."

This time we went into the lounge and sat in slightly more neutral surroundings. "Carry on then," I prompted. "What happened next?"

"Then I got a message from her, she had gone to Mars. She said that she was sorry, but Mike had made her go, had threatened her. She couldn't come back. She said that Mike had a book, and that there was more, he was renting out a room for people to get a bit of privacy, talk, have sex, whatever; but he was filming them, she had found out and he had said that if she didn't go, or if she grassed him up, then she would suffer."

The hole in the wall; that explained it. "Did you confront him?"

"Of course I did, but he just laughed at me, cocky bastard told me to prove it or shut up. He actually dared me to find anyone who would admit to being in there."

He was right, the whole point was that it was secret; you'd hardly go admitting it.

"So I said that I'd tell the miners whose wives he'd been screwing, he laughed again, said that it was such common knowledge that no-one would take any notice, he said that I had nowhere to turn, that he had something on everyone. And that no-one would thank me anyway; he was merely providing a service."

Poor Heynrik, he was so out of his league.

"Then I told him I would tell Munro and that seemed to stop him, he advised me not to but I could tell he wasn't so happy, the cockiness had gone."

"So you went to Munro?"

"Oh yes, I was angry. I'd lost my girl and the arrogant bastard was saying that there was nothing I could do about it. I went straight to him, told him everything."

"What did Munro say?"

"That Mike was a small fish in a big pond, that he would be getting his just deserts and that I wasn't to worry about it. Mike left two days later. I thought it was Munro; I went to thank him and he shrugged and said that he had nothing to do with it."

That was quite a story and could have been complete rubbish for all I knew. It told me a little that I didn't already know, it gave a lot more reason for the desperation of some to get hold of the book but it also gave Heynrik a motive to harm Mike. Even to kill him.

He might have been a good kisser but he wasn't very good with relationships. He hadn't seemed to be in such a state when I had first met him. And why hadn't he got Morgana to come back when Mike left? All the talk about my dress and hair could be a load of bull. I would have to delicately ask Lou how their dates had gone.

"I think you'd better leave," I said.

He got up. "Look, I'm really sorry about how tonight turned out, it wasn't what I had planned. I was over her and over what had happened, especially after I realised that mine wasn't the only life that Mike had messed with. In a way it made me feel less useless to know that it had happened to others. But coming in here and being next to the room where…" he stopped for a second, "…then a drink or two with you reminding me of what we used to do and it all started going around in my head. You went and I thought, I've got a couple of minutes, I'll just have a quick look."

I could sort of see what he meant, but that didn't change the fact that I felt like I had been used, even though I hadn't been, at least not in the way that I had hoped. It was a small comfort to know that I hadn't been filmed with someone else's partner. No wonder people were driving into rocks and breaking in to try and get their hands on this book.

"I'll speak to my boss," he continued. "It might be better if I stay on the farm for a long while."

At last he had come up with a sensible idea.

He practically ran out. Two minutes later he was back. "Can you unlock the door?" he said sheepishly. We didn't say a word and I only lifted the shutters until there was enough room for him to crawl out; I was buggered if I would give him the satisfaction of walking away.

It was time to get to bed, on my own, and try and work out just what had been going on here. More and more things were being revealed as time went on, the whole station, with a few exceptions, was filled with people looking over their shoulders and this place, my café, was the centre of it all. It took a while for me to sleep. I felt remorse for not doing what I had intended and keeping things platonic, but at least I hadn't found Heynrik searching for the book after we had done the deed. That would have been worse.

My last waking thought was to wonder, if it had been Derek with me tonight instead of Heynrik, would he have been interested in me or in the book. Maybe it was time for me to find out.

Chapter 30

Cy crept back in at six, he tried to come in quietly but I was in the kitchen and heard him. In the end, I hadn't slept more than a few minutes. I was too wound up. At half past four I had given up, got up and had a shower. Then I started making things. My mum always reckoned that if you were angry your cakes rose better, something to do with the effort you put into it. Perhaps pretending that the mixture was Heynrik made me beat it faster, it certainly splashed it up the walls.

"In here," I called. He walked through.

"I feel more knackered than you look," he said, giving me a hug. "Mind you, I've had a bit of sleep." He leered, "Where's lover boy then, you worn him out?"

"It's a long story, as it turned out Heynrik was more interested in your drawers than mine."

He looked puzzled. "You mean he's…? But I thought he fancied you, and he's been out with Lou."

"No, he's not; well he might be a bit of both but I caught him in your room, searching in the chest."

He hugged me again. "Bloody hell, I'm sorry, Andi, so was he just after the book?"

I started to grizzle, I couldn't help it. Cy said nothing, just wrapped his huge arms around me, like some sort of bear and let me get it all out of my system. The contact felt good, it felt like it should have been last night, sort of right. At that moment I loved Cy more than I could ever admit, he was always there, and he never let me down. It was a shame that things were the way they were. We stayed like that for a while and Cy's shirt got very damp.

"He says that he wasn't to start with but that changed, and I've found out something else."

"What's that?"

"We thought that Morgana left because of her fling with Mike."

"Yes," he said, "that's what the girls said. Is there another reason then?"

"Well according to Heynrik, Morgana was forced to leave because she found out what Mike's side project was."

"And what was that?"

I told him about the hole and the accusations of video blackmail. He went into the spare room and returned with the bits of metal that I had dismissed. "I wondered about these," he said. "I thought maybe it was some sort of broken cooking thing, like a spit on a barbeque but I couldn't figure it out. Now I can see what it was." He clicked the pieces together and they made a tripod, two long legs, one short one and a flat plate on the top.

"Watch," he said, carrying the whole lot to my bathroom. He rested the short leg on the loo seat and the two longer legs touched the floor right under the hole. The plate was now at hole level. "There, he puts the camera on here, wedges the lens in the hole and turns it on. Perfect, he can leave it to record, sound and all. Then he can come back and edit it all later."

The sneaky bastard, as if chasing women wasn't enough, he had to target the station's wife-swappers as well.

"Now we need to find the memory cards, or the camera itself." Cy was as indignant as me, chasing and seducing bored women was one thing, filming infidelity for profit was a bit too much. No wonder so many people were worried by the idea of a book.

"We'll have to decipher the bloody book; I'll bet it's all in there. Get started, Cy. Don't bother coming into the café, just stay out here and get it done."

He nodded. "Until we do we're never gonna get any peace are we?"

"Aren't you tired, Cy?"

"Yeah but I'm awake now, I can always have a snooze later if I'm off café duties." He went into his room and slammed the door.

I got back to getting ready to open up, and prepared to face the throng without crying again.

Chapter 31

That plan failed miserably, Maz came into the café and spotted it immediately, she ran over and hugged me. "Oh dear," she said sympathetically. "The evening didn't go too well, did it?"

"No," I replied, a bit curtly and she stepped back.

"I'm sorry, Maz, I didn't mean to snap. No, it didn't go at all like I expected."

She bustled around. "I've made coffee," she said after a couple of minutes in which I'd tried to compose myself. "Let the crowd wait for a while. You sit here and get it all out."

I told her everything, well except for parts of the snog-fest, and when I got to the part about the reasons for Morgana's departure I realised that I had said more than I intended. Bloody teachers again.

"It seems to me," said Maz, "that Mike was in over his head, I suspect that Munro persuaded him to leave, despite what he said." She gave me the teacher truth stare. "Are you looking for the book?"

I debated what to say as the eyes bored into me, I felt twelve again, caught doing something.

"We are," I answered, "and when we find it, I'm going to burn it, unopened, in front of everyone in this place, and then perhaps we can get some peace."

"That's a nice idea," she said, "but I suspect that you wouldn't get the chance. I'd heard a little of what you just told me; and I was here when they had a big argument. I could hear them shouting while I was serving. When Heynrik asked you out I wondered about his intentions, but I didn't want to spoil your evening."

So she could have saved me the grief. I just looked at her.

"The station teaches you to be careful about how much of what you know you share," she said. "It's the overcrowding thing. Any way it was none of my business, looking back, I'm sorry but then everyone always gets it right looking back."

What she said was so true, I couldn't be angry with her. Meggie appeared and went straight into the kitchen; she muttered, "Hi," as she passed but never mentioned my date, which was a relief.

We opened up and I hid behind the coffee machine while Maz did the customer relations bit, Claire came in and was about to ask me how things had gone, Maz shook her head and she diplomatically left me alone.

Then Lou arrived, she shoved her way past Maz and grabbed me. "What did you do to him?" she practically screamed in my ear.

Maz had recovered and stepped in. "She had a bad evening, Lou," she said. "Best leave her be."

But Lou wasn't having any of that. "The inspection squad found Heynrik in the stairwell this morning; he's tried to hang himself!"

I think that I must have fainted, the next thing I remembered was Cy's face, it was so close that I couldn't focus on it. "She's awake," he said.

I sat in the lounge, drinking hot chocolate; Claire had found out from the infirmary that Heynrik was still alive, although he was in a coma. So he wouldn't be saying much for a while.

Security had come to see me; Heynrik was carrying a note, which I had been allowed to see. It didn't mention the book, or Mike, he just apologised for embarrassing me, he said that I had reminded him of a previous relationship and he had got emotional. He said that things had got too much for him and that he couldn't stand living any more but that I wasn't to blame.

That should have made me feel better but somehow it didn't.

Lou and Terri, after Lou's outburst, were supportive. Maz must have spoken to them because they both came in and tried to comfort me. Lou apologised for her outburst. I wondered how much of my story Maz had actually told them so I said very little. In the end they left. I was alone with my thoughts, shocked by the way things had turned out. I'd never considered how Heynrik felt; I'd only thought his actions to be manipulative.

I felt guilt at stirring up emotions in him but as Cy said, they must have been there all the time. The rest of the day passed in a blur, Davina came in and saw my face. "Heynrik was a creep," she said. "I never knew what Morgana saw in him anyway, Dad heard about it this morning, he says that he's sorry to hear what's happened; if you want to talk anytime you know where he is." I thought that was sweet, she didn't know that all the time I was with Heynrik I had wanted to be with Derek; I really would have to make the effort, even if it was potentially awkward. At least Davina didn't warn me off her father.

For the next few hours I just sat, a collection of full cups and plates started to grow around me. I couldn't function. No matter how much I knew that I hadn't, and everyone kept telling me, I couldn't stop thinking that it was me who had pushed him over the edge.

Liz came to see me mid-afternoon; Cy had called the pharmacy for advice. She took one look and gave me a sleeping pill. It was only 4 p.m. but I was asleep almost before my head hit the pillow.

Chapter 32

I woke, what time was it, where was I? Then I remembered. My head felt like it was full of cotton wool and I needed the loo. As I sat I heard a squeak. It must be morning, the pill had knocked me out and I had slept through, what time was it? It sounded like someone was in the storeroom, boxes were being shifted and then I heard the fridge door squeak again where I still hadn't oiled it. Good old Cy, he must be up and covering for me with the girls.

I went back into the washroom and flicked the light on, it was only five thirty. Cy wouldn't be up and working. So who was in the store?

Not someone else after the book? I was getting fed up with all the attention; I might as well open the door and offer anyone the chance to search for whatever they thought was here. At least we could get it all done in office hours and not while I was trying to sleep or get laid.

Whoever it was, they wouldn't give up. No time for straighteners, I needed Cy and his ladle. I slipped into my overalls and crept to the door. The noise was definitely coming from the storeroom, and it had a big strong door. I crept down the passageway, grabbed the handle and swung it shut. Quickly, I turned the key, locking our prowler inside. There was a muffled shout, and then the door handle rattled. Ha! I thought, get out of that.

Now I had to get Cy and a couple of hunky security guards for when the door opened. I was about to turn when I felt a hand on my shoulder. Oh crap, there were two of them! I froze for a second. The hand was on my right shoulder, instead of turning into it I went the other way, ducking as I did so.

"Lovely moves, Andi."

"Bloody hell, Cy, you scared the life out of me!"

He had a baseball bat and a fetching silk dressing gown on. "I borrowed this from the lads at the farm; it's much manlier than a ladle. What are you doing, creeping around? You should be zonked."

"I thought that there was another one," I explained. He looked quizzical, then a thumping started on the door. "We'll have to call security this time."

I went into the café and used the phone by the counter. The place was in darkness, the only light coming through the ports from the planet. There were deep shadows and I imagined all sorts of accomplices hiding as I made the call. They said they would be two minutes and not to open the front door until I saw the flashing lights from their run-around.

The door; I looked and it was wide open, the shutter was up as well, someone had worked around the new codes on both locks. Just then I saw the reflection of a flashing blue light in the windows. It was a security run-around.

There were two of them, full body armour and ready to fight off the ravening hordes. I do like a man in uniform though. "Hello, Miss Pett," said the taller one, I'd seen him before. "What's your problem?" He didn't say 'this time', but maybe he thought it.

"There's someone in the storeroom, I've locked him in."

"Leave it to us," they said and walked straight to it, they must have known where it was. Maybe they had been regular visitors when Mike was in charge, rescuing him from angry husbands.

Cy moved out of the way as they opened the door.

The room looked empty; they both moved inside and split up to search between the racks.

I had the sudden vision of a figure, dressed all in black with a mask on, pushing past one of them and making a dash for the door. He shoved me aside as they shouted at them to stop.

As I sprawled in a most unladylike manner across the floor, he leapt over me and through the doorway into the café, straight into Cy's bat. He collapsed like a sack of potatoes and Cy grinned, he sat on the body; that would stop it moving too far.

The guards had caught up. "That was unnecessary, sir," one said. "We had the situation under control."

"He was getting away," said Cy, standing up.

The second pulled out a Taser. "He wouldn't have got far, and anyway we had a man on the entrance."

I went back into the café and sure enough, there was a third guard by the door. He wasn't dressed in full armour like the other two. He nodded to me.

I wanted to know who was sneaking around and how they had got in.

"Did you lower the shutters and lock up, Cy?" I asked him.

"Course I did," he said.

I went over to the prone figure, who was being cuffed. I could see a really bad burn on their wrist, it still had flecks of material in the scabs, so this was the one who had broken in before. I bent to pull off the mask.

He was blonde and clean shaven; definitely the same one Terri and I had chased. Close up, I was even more certain that I had seen him before.

"Will you have a look to see if anything's missing," said one of the guards. They picked blondie up between them and dragged him out to their run-around. "We'll be in touch," one said as they closed the door. And they were gone.

I locked up again and turned the lights out. My head was clearing slowly but even though I wasn't operating flat out there was something about the episode that didn't quite ring true to me.

"Did any of that seem funny to you?" I asked Cy.

"Most of it," he replied. "They seemed uninterested in who he was or in what had happened."

"That's what I thought, I did wonder if it was because I was still a bit groggy from the pill."

"Nope," he confirmed my suspicions. "Total disinterest, as if they were just tidying up, not investigating a crime."

There was something else that nagged at my mind, something that felt weird about the whole thing. I couldn't work it out. "I'm going back to bed," I muttered.

Cy must have stayed up and got us organised, at eleven he woke me with tea and toast. "You feeling better now?" he asked.

"A bit, is everything OK with the café?"

"That's not as important as you are," he said. "But since you ask, Maz and Claire have got it all running smoothly, they said not to worry. And now that Meggie's doing breakfasts as well it's all sorted, eat your toast." He left me to it.

As I ate my toast it came to me, there were definitely only two of them in the run-around when it arrived, they only had two seats. So where did the third one spring from? I mulled that over for a while.

Cy returned and showed me his contribution to the puzzle. "I got this from our friend; I saw it sticking out of his pocket when he dropped. I sat on him so I could get it without being too obvious." He passed me a small box.

"What is it?" I asked.

"It's a radio, the same as Munro's men had, you know when they first came to see us."

That was it, the three men in black with Munro; he had been one of them. He hadn't looked like a henchman; he had even blushed at something. "That's where I saw him before, Cy; he was with Munro, the first day."

"That's right, two hunks and him; he looked like he was in the wrong place." He paused as he caught up to where I was.

"Do you think…?"

I remembered the way Munro had dealt with the fight in the café, how he had persuaded the guards to back down. "Yes."

Cy nodded. "I do too, who do you reckon the guards really answer to? I have a sneaking suspicion that this was a semi-official visit, looking for the book. I reckon there were two of them, one in the storeroom and one looking out. We disturbed one and the other hid until the guards turned up, then he became the third one."

"That all makes sense."

"That's not all," Cy said with a grin, "after what Heynrik said, I looked in the book again. The rear cover was split open; under the hasp thing, there was sheet of cardboard in it."

"Did it have the key to the code on it?"

"No, but it had several memory cards, in slots cut out of it."

Now that was progress. "Have you tried to play them?"

"Yes and they're password protected, but here's the kicker, all the file names are ten characters long, in the same code!"

Now that was interesting.

Chapter 33

Munro walked into the café. "Can I have a word, Miss Pett?" he asked. I'd been expecting him, ever since we had worked out who the mystery man had been. Davina noticed him and I could see her ears prick up.

"Of course," I said. "Come into the lounge, it's a bit more private, do you want coffee?"

"No, thank you," he replied. "I won't be long but it's important that I talk to you."

We went into the lounge and he sat in one of the armchairs. I was going to wait for him to speak first; I didn't know how he would play it. I shut the door and sat opposite him. "What can I do for you?"

"It's about your intruder, I'm sure you have realised that the man they caught, Gordie Coombs, was one of the men who accompanied me when I welcomed you."

I nodded. "I had spotted that, and there was this." I threw him the radio Cy had found.

"Thank you," he said, as he put it in his pocket. "Let me tell you, honestly, that he was not acting on my orders, I have no interest in burglary. I do hope that this is not taken the wrong way but you have nothing that I desire. And you mustn't forget that I had the run of this place between Mike's departure and your arrival."

That was true, he sounded sincere, but then, all of the best ones did.

"Gordie was a junior member of my staff; he was alone on the station. His parents had been on a short term contract and left. He wanted to stay and I agreed to look after him for them. I suspect that he did what he did because he thought it might impress me, there had been talk around the station about something of value that Mike might have left here." He paused. "Although I imagine that anything like that would have left with him."

"Thank you for your honesty, I appreciate it." I wasn't going to slip up and let him know that I knew what he knew; or something like that. Anyway, I kept away from the subject of books.

"He was persistent though, I burned him the first time. I'm surprised he came back."

Munro either didn't know that or he played a lot of poker. "I wondered how he got that wound, he wouldn't tell me; was it you?"

"He got on the wrong end of my hair straighteners," I explained.

He winced, just like Cy had. "You're clearly not someone to mess with." He paused for a second, "You know, someone like you could fit into my organisation very well." Now there was an offer; could I refuse?

"I'll have to think about that."

He nodded. "Of course, there's no rush, take your time."

"What will happen to this Gordie now?"

Munro adopted a sad expression. "He will appear in front of the council, but that's just a formality, he can hardly dispute the facts. He will be given a chance to plead; the guards will want him out of the way. He'll be deported to Mars to stand trial for his crimes."

"And you won't stop that, you seemed keen enough to intervene with the guards when it suited you?"

"That's exactly what I like about you; you cut straight through the bull. No, I pick my interventions very carefully. The argument in your café, that was a low risk thing, there is a fear of the power of the mining union and I played on that. It would make me popular, like Robin Hood. But where a man has been caught red-handed, thanks to you very red-wristed as well, then if I said too much it might force people to question my motives, especially if it were found that he works for me."

Not only was he a megalomaniac, he was a psychologist and a

deep thinker as well. That was why he was so successful.

He rose. "Well, it's been lovely to chat but I have things to do."

"Running your evil empire?"

He laughed. "Come and work for me, Andi. I won't bite and you'll end up very well off. Talk to your partner, tell him what I said, he may be interested even if you're not."

I had my doubts. "I'll let you know," I said opening the door. Davina was walking away; it looked like she had just come from the bathroom, why hadn't she used the one in the café?

"The lovely Davina," Munro said. "It's such a pity." He said no more and walked briskly away.

Munro was calling in his favour; did he want me to work for him because I was getting closer to the truth? I didn't think so, but then I wouldn't always recognise the truth if I fell over it.

Chapter 34

Cy was searching the stores again, for the umpteenth time, this time for the camera. He lifted all the boxes down from the high shelves again, and I looked inside them, again. Really, this was getting tedious. We moved to the other room and looked in the fridges, again. We had talked about a bit of light exhumation; it was looking more and more likely that we would have to see if the camera was in with the corpse.

He walked past the letter 'L', covered in dust; absently he kicked out at it. It went flying across the floor, landing with a thump against the fridge. A bulb shattered. "Cy," I said, "careful, I might want to put that back."

He went to pick it up. "The back's come off, there's nothing in there though, just wiring."

I had a lightbulb moment. "The 'L'. It's missing from the sign. What about if that's the key to the code."

He stopped still for a second, as he realised what I meant. "It could be, I'm getting nowhere fast."

"What about if you go to L?"

He grinned. "That's not very nice, and we're supposed to be friends."

"Base everything on L, you know what I mean."

He practically ran back to his room. An hour later he came out, with a triumphant expression.

"I've got it, you were right."

"Was I?"

He grabbed me and kissed me, he must have been excited. "It's the key to the code, L is the key. Andi, you're a genius."

Why had he taken so long to realise that? I'd been telling him for years.

"If you start the alphabet in the book at L, change every L to an A and so on, it all makes sense. I've already done a couple of pages; it's not perfect but it works."

This was fantastic. "And what does it say?"

"Come into my room and I'll show you."

Cy spread the sheets out on his desk. "Here are the copies of the coded pages, and once you substitute A for L it all makes sense. There are still a few things to sort out, punctuation, numbers and spacing; I've had to sort out the blocks of letters. I did the first page, and then I skipped and chose a page at random. If you want me to do any more I'll get quicker as I get used to it."

What did he mean, if I wanted more? I wanted to know everything. I read the first page, then the second, and then I understood what he meant.

Chapter 35

If you're reading this, then I'm dead and my insurance policy hasn't worked. Well done for working out why I never put the L back up.

I'm Mike, or at least I was when I wrote this. I came to the station for a change. I certainly got that.

When I first started running the Lucky Strike, I needed staff to be able to offer twenty-four hour service and found some bored and lonely women on the station who were willing to work for me. It turned out that there were more of them than I had realised and that some were willing to do more for me than others. Before I knew where I was the fringe benefits made their appearance. The working men on here worked hard, in a dangerous and demanding job. Their women, who had come out here to spend time with them, found that they hardly ever saw them. When they did they were tired and either wanted to get drunk and wind down or just sleep until they had to work again. And that's where I came in. I was available for a chat; I was never more interested in a few beers and a sleep than I was in them, and that made them happy.

I looked up at Cy. "Not what I was expecting. As an insurance policy it hadn't worked that well then, had it?"

"No," he agreed. "But the tone soon changes." I went back to the sheet; in a different pen he had added more.

I only started this journal so that I could keep up with what I was doing. All I ever intended was to be a listener, someone who people could talk to. In my innocence I thought that would be enough. But it turned out that the women had other ideas. Before I knew it I was doing more than just talking. And that was where life started to get complicated. And I suppose that the first one told her friends, or perhaps they noticed her change of mood and asked her what was different. Soon I was getting requests. It turned into a bit of private fun, scoring and comparing. Then I started to get visits from husbands and boyfriends and I realised that it would have to stop. But it was one thing me wanting to stop, my customers weren't so keen. That's when I saw the benefit of this book and started keeping proper video records as well. I made the hole in the wall, and the tripod. So that if I needed to, I could show my side of the story. It's not just men who take what they want, sometimes it's women. And some of them were prepared to sacrifice me to cover up for their own choices. They told me that I would have to do what they wanted, that I was trapped. So I made sure that they were trapped too. And then I got involved in something else.

This was dynamite, I looked across at Cy. "See what I mean?" he asked.

"Just let me read it, Cy." I picked up the other page that Cy had decoded.

My first paying client for the spare room today. The first time it wasn't me in there, I was behind the camera this time, instead of the star. It all happened so quickly. One of my ladies, one of the less complicated ones, mentioned that her friends were desperate for a place to hide out, neighbours and husbands were getting suspicious and did I think I could lend them the spare room here for the odd afternoon. So I wasn't the only one doing what I was doing, the knowledge gave me comfort. I was still trying to reduce my activities, if the room was full I could hardly use it myself, I hoped this would help.

And anyway, it seemed such a reasonable request that I

was happy to comply. When I saw who it was I realised that there might be more to it than just the desire for a bit of afternoon delight. The lady was a member of the council and her beau a senior mining manager. They were publicly engaged in negotiations about the uses of the station and who profited from what. The threat of strike action and all that entailed for the station was very real. The day after their tryst, before I'd had a chance to look at the video, a deal was announced. When they had left, they had thanked me for my discretion and told me they had credited my account. They asked if they could use the room again. For the money they were paying me I was more than happy. A week later they were back, I'd had a chance to see the video and apart from the sex, it was all boring talk, legal and technical stuff that I didn't understand.

Mike wrote in a strange, pedantic style; it gave him character. "This is dynamite, Cy, we need to know more."

"The titles on the pages were in the same code," he said. "You know how they were all the same length." I nodded. "Well that's because they were all video file titles, the camera that created them must have named them all like that."

"And we have the files?"

"Yes, they're the same as the files on the memory cards. Each file is probably a record of whatever went on in the room. The page is just a summary."

"Good work, Cy. We'll worry about them later, for now just get a few more pages decoded."

"Where are we going with this, Andi? Do we really need to do more? Surely we have enough here to go to the guards. This isn't just bonking now, we could be dealing with industrial espionage, secret deals, plots, who knows what."

I had promised Terri that I wouldn't delve too deeply, but that was when I thought it was just a list of conquests. That had all changed. And it turned out that it wasn't just Mike preying on bored women, they had been doing a bit of preying themselves.

Chapter 36

I had an official envelope in the internal mail; I assumed it would be about Heynrik or the break-in so I was surprised when I opened it to find it was from the mining company.

I was even more surprised to find that I had been invited to be examined for the position of Scooper pilot, and it was the same afternoon. It had been sitting in the admin office for a week, probably next to my electrician's job sheet.

"Bloody hell," Cy said when I told him. "You're going to be a Scooper pilot?"

"Don't mock until you've tried it," I said, on top of everything else that had been going on I had forgotten all about my application. As well as the café, and Cy's ongoing decoding, I had been down to see Heynrik in the infirmary most days, he was still unconscious and they had no idea if he would ever recover. I had spent hours holding his hand, telling him I was sorry how things had worked out. Just talking in the hope that a voice might wake him up.

I had only read the documentation once or twice, I had never revised for an exam and I wasn't going to start now. But I still presented myself in the workshop, ready to have a go.

"All ready?" asked Tina.

"I only got the letter this morning; I thought I had to do more flying before I could be tested."

"Bloody admin," she was annoyed. "Why can't they just deliver the internal post? You need to do four hours and you've done two in the simulator already. So we can do two more today and then I can test you on the procedures. You have read everything?" I made a noise that could have meant anything, she chose to assume it meant yes.

So this was it, no more simulation, we went down to the hangar in the secure lift. This time we ignored the simulator and went to a different Scooper, still fitted with two seats. Tina put me in the driving seat and told me to go through the same routine as I had done in the simulator. "We're Scooper 2, for the radio," she said as I tried to start up the engines. Nothing happened. "You haven't disconnected the fuel and gas lines," she said.

"Have I failed already?"

She laughed. "Everyone forgets, it's because you don't have to do it on the simulator. Just press and turn." I got back out and unhooked us. That had broken the ice and relaxed me. I managed to do everything else in the right order. When we drifted into the airlock it was just like it had been on the simulator.

The Scooper was identical in every respect, except that it actually moved. "This is the exam," Tina told me as we waited for the air to be pumped out. "I'm not your friend today, I'm the examiner and you'd better do it properly cos everyone will be watching. If you pass you'll be put on the reserve list, when there's a vacancy you'll be offered the extra training. Pass that and you can have a job."

"Fine," I said. I was excited at the prospect of actually going out in space. I checked my straps were tight.

"Clive's not very happy; he's in charge of the drivers. But then he's not the only examiner, I'm one and I made sure I got you today. If I say you're safe he can moan but there's nothing he can do. Chandler's happy, he likes you and he's a bigger boss than Clive. Once you're on the reserve list, you'll be allowed to go out on your own, when you want, as long as there's a spare Scooper and you don't get in the way. You can't mine until you've done the extra training but you can use one for leisure. A lot of people use them for picnics or rock-hopping, you can always mount an extra seat in one if you want."

"Thanks, Tina. I appreciate you doing this for me."

"Are you ready then?" she asked as the meter dropped towards zero.

"Sure, it feels just the same." The door opened, I called Control again and we left the safety of the station. I was flying, for real, and there was somewhere I wanted to go.

"Can I do something first?" I asked.

"As long as it doesn't involve anything stupid, like trying to drive into the café." Tina must have read my mind, sort of.

"I want to look at the station close-up from the outside."

"That's fine, just don't bump into it, stay ten metres away, the alarm will sound if you get any closer."

I swung around and closed on the bulk of the station. Each deck was marked with broad bands of windows; I counted and rose till I was level with the café. I drove around until I found it, there was my bedroom port, I remembered thinking that no-one would ever be looking in on me. Moving on I saw the picture windows of the café, I could just make out people sitting, eating and drinking like it was normal. Maybe it was and at this moment I was the abnormal one. I rose up again, past the observation level and the windowless farm. Here was the telescope and the dome of the observatory. I zoomed over to it but couldn't see inside through the tinted glass.

"OK, I'm done," I said.

"Nice controlled flying," Tina praised me, that didn't happen very often and I basked. I lost concentration, my foot pressed the pedal and we headed straight towards the dome. I hauled on the wheel and we missed it by a good whisker. Tina gripped the back of my seat.

"We'll forget that bit," said Tina, as I slowed down. "Now do what you're told."

She gave me instructions on where to head and we accelerated toward Saturn, away from the mining operation. The planet started to fill the screens as we approached. She told me to turn and I spun the wheel, we stopped and looked back at the station.

Inside it seemed so big; when I drove past my café and up the side of it, it had seemed even bigger. Now out here, even though we were no more than a few thousand metres away from it, it had become a speck. It had lights but they merged with the stars and as I had found out once, if you weren't keeping your eye on it, you'd miss it. No wonder I'd lost myself on the simulator. At least I knew now that I could press the auto-return on the computer and the machine would find its own way back.

Tina called Control. "Scooper 2, part one of the test on Andorra Pett is complete, we're going radio silent for a few moments while I explain the test procedures for part two." Control answered and Tina turned the radio off. "Now I've got you on your own," she said. "We need to talk."

This sounded ominous. "About?"

"Mike, it broke my heart when I found out that he was lying there in your freezer. It's been eating me up, I need to know who and why. I know you're doing the same thing, looking for answers; have you found the book yet?" She was agitated, and I guess that was what she had been taking out on the metal that day in the workshop.

"Am I in danger from you, Tina? Are you in the book?"

"Hell no," she laughed. "Do you think that I killed him? I loved him! And nobody knows. Yes I'm in there. People think that I couldn't possibly be in the book, because I'm Tina the welder and he was only interested in the pretty ones, the thin ones, like you and the twins. Is being out here with me worrying you? I just wanted a bit of privacy to ask if you'd found the book."

It was so sad, Tina might not have been conventional but to think that she wasn't pretty was just wrong. "I'm not exactly thin, Tina," I said. "And anyone who thinks that you can't be pretty unless you are is a bit deluded."

"I could hear them talk in the Strike," she continued. "I'd sit there, on my own with a beer and they would chatter over their skinny drinks, about who'd lost the most grams and how much more attractive it made them; about how Mike would compliment them. And I wanted to shout, it's not important, he compliments my curvy bits, can't you *see*? It's what he says! I knew he was shagging all of them as well but I knew that from the start. It didn't matter. He made me, fat weird Tina the welder, feel special, even if it was only for a while."

I had to tell someone what Cy and I were doing; it might as well be Tina. She wasn't how she described herself but she could be the only person I could really confide in. "Are you sure that radio's turned off?"

"Yes, look." She pointed to the switch.

"OK," I nodded. "Yes we found the book but it's in code, and we've found out more as well. You know about the women but not all the details, there's so much more to it than anyone thinks. Mike wasn't just blackmailing women; they were blackmailing him as well. And he was renting the spare room behind the café for a safe place for people to have illicit sex. That's bad enough but he was filming it all. He was playing everyone off against everyone else."

She looked shocked. "We all knew he was up to all sorts of stuff but not that. We all thought he was just servicing bored women. Does that mean he filmed *me*? Have you told anyone official?"

"Not yet, we have the memory cards with the video and the book itself. We don't know all of it, like who's on the video. I certainly don't want to watch any of it; it's not my thing at all. We wanted to decipher the book before we did anything. And until we've read it all, we don't know who's involved. Who do we go to?"

She thought for a moment. "I see what you mean, what are you going to do then?"

That was the big question. "Is it really worth destroying all those lives, hasn't there been enough disruption?"

She thought about it. "Well, there are some guilty ones who need exposing, the ones who think they've got away with it. Everyone else has had their lives destroyed already. And what about all the ones who are presumed guilty but just might be innocent; surely they deserve a chance to be vindicated?"

That was all true. "I suppose that they've suffered enough, all those suspicious husbands and worried wives. They deserve closure."

As always it was a balancing act, whose need was the greatest? I knew what I thought was a good idea.

"I think that the best plan will be to destroy the book and then tell everyone that we've done it."

Tina shook her head. "That won't help. No-one will believe you didn't read it, or that you won't have kept a copy. If people were paying Mike, they might think now that you have the evidence; it might all start again, that they'll be paying you. And if the murderer is still out there…"

She was right, and I could see her point, then what could we do? "You're the only other person who knows that we've found it," I told her. "Please don't spread it around; we've had enough excitement as it is."

"What else has happened? I know about the break-in and Raf getting earache."

"We've had two break-ins, and Cy's been injured trying to stop a fight, when I crowned Raf. I thought I was on a promise with Heynrik but it turned out that he was after the book and not me, then he went and did what he did. I don't know if I can put up with much more."

"Well, none of the miners are talking about the book any more, not even Clive. The general consensus is that whoever did what, it's all over now. Mike's gone and life has got back to normal. I'm sorry to disappoint but you're not seen as a threat, they say you're cute but too feisty, I think that when you stood up to Clive and battered Raf it scared a few of them."

"We still need to catch the murderer, and then we can find the body. Then peace will reign, the book won't matter and everyone will live happily ever after."

"Do you have any ideas on how you're going to do all that?"

"I'm keeping my ears open; sooner or later whoever it is will slip up."

Tina turned the radio back on. "Control, this is Scooper 2, we're running part two of a test on Andorra Pett, record for competency evaluation please."

Control acknowledged the message. Tina went back into professional mode. "Right then, now that's out of the way you can show me your moves."

Two hours later I guided the Scooper back into the airlock. I was drenched with sweat and my arms ached from hauling on the controls. I had thought that they were minimal, now I knew why, any more things to push or turn and you would have had a brain overload.

Tina had directed me into the stream of rocks that the miners used. "We're geo-stationary over the planet," she said. "But the stream still moves. The miners go with the flow and scoop little rocks from the edge. So to start with, you do that."

I moved towards the rocks and they seemed to speed up as I approached. Tentatively I dipped the Scooper's basket under a rather pathetic pebble and lifted the nose. As it sank into the mesh I turned away from the stream.

"Nice," Tina said. "Delicately done, you've just scooped your first rock. Normally there would be a collector behind us for you to dump it into. The lever opens the bottom of the basket. Or you can do the opposite of what you did to catch it and nudge it along. But you can go and try for a bigger one now."

I turned back into the jostling flow of rocks and selected a much bigger piece. It was milky white and pockmarked, rotating slowly as I matched its speed and grabbed it in the basket. As I tried to turn away, I found myself unable to do so. I hauled on the wheel and pressed the pedal, alarms sounded. It was like I had grabbed a mountain and tried to carry it away in my hands. "What do I do?"

Tina laughed. "Don't panic, that's the first thing, just ease the power off."

I lifted my foot and the alarms stopped. I still had the rock in the basket, it was still moving in the stream and I felt it tug at the Scooper. Tina didn't seem bothered so I tried not to be.

"Good, now the reason that all went wrong is that you were trying to change the inertia of the rock."

Now that we had no power I felt the Scooper being dragged along by the weight of the rock. It swung and bumped against another rock, the rubber fenders taking most of the impact, still we bounced about a bit.

"Sorry, Tina. You lost me at 'the reason'. I run a café, remember." I was struggling to keep hold of my breakfast, we were rolling and pitching, the collisions seemed dangerous, surely we would split open and die horribly. Did people do this for twelve hours at a time? I viewed the miners with a bit more respect; no wonder some of them were a bit edgy.

On top of that, if they thought that their ladies were messing around, it would be enough to spoil their concentration, if they thought it was with someone who didn't do this sort of work, who had a soft job, one where they had a good chance of avoiding a horrible death, I could see the anger.

"OK," said Tina, "put simply then, the rock wants to keep going and you want to move it. The rock has been doing its thing for a long time, it's built up what we call inertia, think of it like skating, when you try and change direction your body wants to keep going in a straight line."

I thought about my attempts at ice skating with Trevor.

"My body just wants to fall on its arse! But I see what you mean." At last she wasn't being too patronising.

"So we have to persuade it to change direction, and we do that by moving it gently. Now we've dropped in behind the rock, it's dragging us along. So if you spin the wheel as far as it will go to the right and give it about half power, well... just try it."

I did and we sort of drove around the rock until we were at an angle to it. Now we were inside the stream. More rocks bumped,

Tina gave me instructions and I put on more power, slowly the rock moved clear of the stream.

"At that wheel setting all the thrust is trying to get us to nudge the rock sideways, out of the flow," she explained. "We don't have enough power to use brute force; we have to use its own inertia to help us."

We started to move clear, picking up speed, quicker and quicker. "Reduce power and centre the wheel." I did and we slowed. "Now you have control, you can carry the rock where you want, but don't forget, as you move it, you give it more inertia; if you want to change its direction you're gonna have to do it slowly. Look at your fuel level."

I glanced down; I had used twenty per cent of my Scooper's fuel just moving that one rock.

"You wouldn't normally go for one that big, a cutter would come in and turn it into lots of little ones for you. But it illustrates the point."

This inertia was a tricky beggar. "Why didn't you show me this on the simulator?"

"It can't replicate this, too many variables. This is why we have the extra training and the practical exam."

Under Tina's instruction and using the auto-return I carried the rock back towards the station, not into the airlock but to a large hopper on the lowest deck. I had to wait in a queue of craft dumping rocks into a big crusher thing, guided by a woman on the radio.

When it was my turn I dipped the basket and backed away, leaving the rock hanging in space. Next I moved forward slowly and nudged it into the hole; it vanished as it met the grinding wheels inside.

"Well done," Tina congratulated me. "That's more than the miners do, the Scoopers collect it and pass it to a carrier, which brings it over here and dumps it. Even so, they still bitch about it all day."

"Is that part of the exam?" I asked. "Because I can bitch on for hours if you like?"

Instead, Tina got me to fly back to the airlock, on the way she asked me a few questions about safety features and radio work, things that I had read about in the paperwork.

It was all very simple, how to send a distress, push the button. How to auto-return, push the other button. What to do if you suffered a pressure leak. Basically the answer to that one was to die horribly unless you could plug it in less than thirteen seconds. There was a box of corks of various sizes under the seat. It looked like the aftermath of a bottle party.

That was it? Two hundred years of space travel, the biggest space station ever made and we had corks if we got a hole in our spaceship. If it hadn't been serious it would be laughable.

As we approached the open airlock, Tina said, "Congratulations, you've passed; we just have to go up to the control room to sign the log and make it all legal."

At that moment, I felt fantastic. I never would have thought how good this would make me feel. I was halfway to being a ring-miner, a job that had a mystique on Earth. What would Trevor, boring old accountant Trevor, think of that!

We left the hangar in the small lift, the same one that Terri had used to get to the observatory. "As you know, this is the secure lift to the control room and all the working spaces," Tina explained. "And now you're a qualified pilot, you'll get your own key-card when we get there."

Chapter 37

I'd never seen so many flashing lights as there were when I got out of the lift in the control room.

Everywhere I looked they winked like so many fireflies, presided over by an army of people, all wearing headsets and talking at once. In the middle of the room was a three dimensional model of the stream, or at least the section that was being worked today. The larger rocks were shown to scale and each had a red tag floating in the air above it. After the strain my mind had just undergone, this was another assault on my senses. To add to the chaos, mining Scoopers were shown as yellow numbered dots, flitting about creating patterns amongst the red. And there were others, all sorts of different colour dots that hovered around.

"What the hell's going on in here, Tina? Are you trying to fry my brains?"

"Come on," she said. "Let's meet the flight duty officer, they can explain."

She took me over to a raised platform at the side of the model; sat there was a uniformed man.

"Hey, Carlos," said Tina to one of the handsomest people I'd seen for, well ever. "This is Andi; she was just flying Scooper 2 for her exam." He turned his stubbled face towards me, brown eyes on full melt. I dove in for a swim in them for a second, then realised that he was talking, to me! I thought it was the sound of leaves rustling in a summer breeze. Honestly, he was that attractive I was polishing my hormones.

"Hello, Tina, Andi," the vision said. "Your rock was a good one, worth just over six thousand, that was."

How did they know? Tina saw my mouth going like a goldfish's and came to my rescue. "I was teaching her about inertia, Carlos," she said. "We never assayed it, I said grab one and she just went for it."

He smiled, showing a full set of dazzling teeth. "Well, you have balls, taking on one that size! Even for beginner's luck it's pretty good, seventeen per cent Dysprosium, you can make a lot of electronics with that."

I fluttered. "It was nothing." Shut up, Andi, stop before you say something stupid about big ones.

"Carlos, can we get Andi logged and registered please?"

"Yeah, I've got a café to run."

"Oh you're that Andi," he smiled. "I've heard all about you."

That was ominous. "You should come down for a coffee sometime," I suggested.

"Thanks," he said, "but I never get chance, sometimes I think I'm the only one who knows how this place runs, and besides, when I'm off duty I like to chill out with Clarissa."

"Pie Clarissa?"

"That's her, she said you were cool, and never to upset you when you're working the milk jug."

And she said you were all she needed, I thought, and now I could understand why. All the good ones were taken.

"I'll set up your registration while Tina shows you around."

I kept my hands in my pockets, in case I touched anything and set off the self-destruct or whatever as Tina took me around the room. The majority of the staff were talking to Scooper drivers or support craft, directing them towards the rocks that showed the most promise.

I watched the model, how did they produce it? I looked up, there were a bank of about fifty screens, showing what the pilots saw. Surveying craft bobbed in and out of the stream, scanning rocks for valuable deposits and the Scoopers grabbed the smaller bits, the bigger rocks were cut up or blown apart by the other craft, the ones I had seen with the strange things hanging off of them.

"How do they get the picture?"

"There are a string of geo-stationary satellites taking video, it's processed and rendered into three dimension real-time graphics." I wish I hadn't bothered asking. Tina carried on in her foreign language. "The graphics are overlaid, green are survey craft, blue utilities like cutters and crackers, yellow for Scoopers and purple for collectors. The rocks are red."

"Hmm…" I said, it sounded like I was absorbing the information, instead of letting it wash over me. Let me sign the form and get back to the café, I thought, I've almost got that worked out.

Tina introduced me to one of the controllers; she was taking a break, sitting in a chair with a cup of coffee. Her headset lay on the arm of the chair. Tina introduced me.

"We have to rest for five minutes every hour or so," she said. "The driver does the same, otherwise you'd burn out, make a mistake."

"So do you have one driver each then," I asked an intelligent question.

"Yeah," she replied. "I get messages in my left ear from the assay and break-up crew; basically they find the good stuff and split it into bits that the Scoopers can handle. They nudge them out of the stream if they can; if not then the Scooper goes in and gets them."

She showed me a handset, like a TV remote. "This updates the status on the model, then everyone can see what's going on."

It sounded complicated, listening and talking at the same time, maybe that was why all the operators I could see were women, multitasking was second nature, we did it all the time when we were shopping.

"So is that all that goes on in here?"

"No, that's just all I do. Hannah over there does the next bit, talk to her, I gotta start again." I thanked her but she was already talking and listening, I could hear the noise from her headset as instructions were relayed to her.

Hannah was sat at a desk, watching a picture of the hopper I had dumped my rock into, a read-out by the side showed all sorts of numbers. She was organising craft who were ready to dump their loads of rock.

"Hi," she said, not looking up. "Excuse me but I have to watch this, just talk."

"Is that where I dumped my rock?"

"Scooper 2," added Tina.

"That was you?" she said. "Yeah, major result, seventeen per cent, whew, the assay must've missed that one. Good wage, you splitting it, Tina?"

I hadn't even thought that I might get paid for this. "Of course," Tina replied. "Fifty-fifty."

"Right," she tapped buttons. "What's your account?" she asked me.

"Andorra Pett, Ucky Strike," I replied. She never said, 'Oh that Andi,' in a way I felt disappointed.

"Money's all there." Wow this place was efficient, pity they couldn't get me an electrician.

"One more person to see," Tina said, guiding me to an oasis of calm. The sign on the desk said Duty Officer. "This is Don; he's in charge of the overall operation of the station."

The station, the whole station, everything, he looked so calm. "So you're Andi," he said, I hadn't even been introduced. "Don't look so worried. I know who you are because Tina logged you in."

"Is this where you watched me in the simulator?" I asked.

He smirked a little. "Yeah that's right; we have a laugh at all the sim flights. Whenever the radio operator hears Scooper 1 we all drop what we're doing, put it on the speaker and the big screen and kick back for a while."

Bloody hell, that was embarrassing. I still remembered the 'Oh God, I'm going to be sick' wail, the fact that I hadn't actually barfed hardly made up for it.

"Don't take it personal," he continued, "we all had to do it. Do you want to see it?"

Funnily enough it didn't appeal to me. I shook my head.

"Never mind then, we can put it on a memory card for you if you like."

No, he still wasn't selling it, but I could get it for Cy, it'd do him for Christmas.

He produced a tablet, with a certificate on it; it said that I was found qualified to fly mining craft. "Sign here," he said. I scrawled my name in the space, before anyone changed their mind.

"That's you all confirmed then," he said. "Well done." He fished in a drawer and handed me a key-card on a lanyard. "That'll get you in the small lift. Don't lose it."

I felt like I was weightless and all-powerful as I swiped it at the lift.

Chapter 38

When I walked back into the café, Maz presented me with a huge cake. It was shaped like a Scooper. "Terri made it," she said. "We knew that Tina was taking you out so we got her to stall you in the control room until we'd made it." I was touched by the effort.

"It was nothing much," I said.

"Well done," Cy said, hugging me. "We all heard that you're a qualified Scooper pilot now, when will you start taking people out on trips?"

"Steady on, I'm only on the reserve list, but you can be first if you like."

"Not to belittle your achievement, but I remember going in your car in London! That's why I'll pass."

"Yes, but this time, Cy, I'm actually allowed to hit things, and I have fenders."

"You could have done with a few of them back then," he said with a grin.

Me, Cy, Maz, Claire, Meggie, Terri and Davina polished off the cake; we even saved a bit for Lou, who was stuck measuring phase shifts, whatever they were. It didn't sound quite as exciting as scooping was turning out to be. I hope I hadn't frightened her; zooming in on the observatory when I'd lost control.

When they had all left, Cy went back to his decoding. "It's going so much quicker now," he said. "I've worked out how he did the spacing between words and that's made it easier. Did you know that if you get the first and last letter, the rest don't have to be in order for your brain to work out the word?"

I didn't know that. "Tina opened her heart out to me today," I said. "She got me on my own in the Scooper, turned the radio off and said we needed to talk."

Cy laughed. "Bet you thought you were in deep shit."

"I did, it all went through my mind, was I with Mike's murderer? But she, like everyone else around here, wanted to know if I had the book."

"Well you're still here. Hang on," he realised what that must mean. "She wasn't, was she?"

He considered for a moment. "Mind you, she's not bad looking, the shaved head and the tattoos might put a few off but she's got a lovely figure. A few curves, something to get hold of, a bit like you."

Coming from Cy that meant more than it would from anyone else. Tina should get to know Cy. It wouldn't be the same as knowing Mike, it would be better; he would bolster her self-esteem without any ulterior motive.

"She was, and when I told her about the video she was worried. You should tell her, about the figure," I suggested. "She feels inadequate around stick insects, like I do."

"Well, you're both daft then; what else did she say?"

"We talked about what we intended to do, whether it was right to read it all, or better to let it lie."

He thought about that and then I told him what Terri had said, about Mike's threats.

"So some of the book might be lies?"

"Except the video, that can't lie."

Cy went quiet as he digested that.

"This doesn't get any less of a moral maze," he replied at last.

Chapter 39

Next morning, Maz arrived as usual; I had decided to quiz her about the blonde man.

"Do you know someone called Gordie, Maz? Blonde hair. Young looking."

"Sure I do," she said. "It's Gordie Coombes; his father is big in the refinery. I heard that he's been arrested." So Munro had lied, he wasn't alone on the station.

"He was the intruder in the café yesterday," I explained, and her usual calm demeanour cracked, just for a second. "Does Davina know?"

"I've no idea, why do you ask?"

"Gordie is Davina's boyfriend," she said matter-of-fact. "Best not to mention it to her."

Cy came out to drag me away from serving. "I've done another load of pages. You have to know this, it's dynamite," he said when we were alone.

"What, Cy?" He dropped the bomb.

"Munro's wife was in here, with one of the miners, there's a video and all sorts."

I knew that Munro had a wife; he had told me that she worked in the farm processing plant, making cakes. Nobody else had ever mentioned her.

"Were they talking or bonking?"

"Both, she was telling him that Munro had heard about plans for neutralising the influence of the miners, and wanted to know if he knew that the farmers wanted to take over the running of the station."

Oh crap, that could give Munro another reason to kill Mike. "And we still can't play the video?"

"No, I haven't found the password yet, I'm just telling you what's in the notes Mike made after watching it. It looks like that was when he decided that silence could be bought."

"And he threatened Munro's wife?"

"I don't know, yet. I'm going as fast as I can on this, Andi, but there are pages of it."

I had an idea. "Cy, can you tell from the pages you haven't decoded which contain more symbols than numbers?"

"Yes, I think so."

"OK, look for a page that has more numbers, it might be a summary of payments and names."

"Got it."

It was time for me to go and see Derek. I'd been wanting to see him until Heynrik had happened; now I wasn't sure of the reception that I'd get.

Chapter 40

I got out of the lift at the lower farm deck and after the spray and a footbath I made my way to the offices. I asked at the desk where I could find Derek, a phone call was made and he appeared out of a glass door. "Hello, Andi," he said. "Please come down to my office, to what do we owe this pleasure?"

I sat in an armchair, his office had a long glass wall that looked over the fields, he sat behind a large overflowing desk. We talked about the fish project; he said that my idea about a mobile tank was promising.

They were waiting on supplies so they could build a larger tank but small scale modelling looked like it might duplicate the conditions in tidal salt water. "Lobster may soon be on the menu," he said with a smile. "Do you want to come down and have a look?"

"Yes, I'd love to; I can't believe that an idea of mine would be any use."

He laughed. "You shouldn't put yourself down, Andi. Why can't your ideas be as good as ours?"

There was a door in the glass wall of Derek's office. "I had that fitted last year, I can sneak about and the secretaries never know when I'm in," he said, my suspicious mind went into overdrive; he could go anywhere and have an alibi. "Come and see the future, we're trying to reduce the luxury imports, become more self-sufficient."

We walked across a courtyard and entered a low building, through a plastic screen. Inside it was humid, I felt my hair frizz; marvellous, if there were any birds in here they would be taking up residence.

"Will you put these on please," he asked; handing me a white coat and a hairnet, plus a pair of white overshoes. "It's a cleanliness thing."

I donned the clothing and we went through another screen into the next room. Banana trees, or was that bushes? grew in huge pots in harsh lighting, there were oranges and other fruits I didn't recognise all jumbled together. It was more like the stock room in a crazy garden centre than a place where food was grown. Other people were working in here; they were dressed in one-piece suits with clear fronted helmets.

"We're due to expand this bit, it's all a bit new and confused at the moment; but the plants all seem to be doing alright, they're very adaptable."

Derek kept up a running commentary as we walked towards the far end of the space. Through another door and we were in a room filled with large tanks. There were big prawns bobbing about in one and I could see fish that looked like trout swimming in another. This tank had a pump at one end and the water was clearly flowing, the fish swam but stayed in the same place.

"This one is halfway to your idea," Derek explained. "We have the water flowing, like in a river, but the goal is for waves, not current."

By the side of these tanks was a smaller one which rocked from side to side, it was a bit ferocious and water splashed. "Now this is your idea," he said. "It's set on hydraulics and the motion simulates the action of waves, if we can create a rocky habitat and fill it with salt water, I think that lobster would love it. We need to make the motion a little less frantic though."

We moved through the buildings and Derek showed me the other experimental work they were doing, he had watercress growing in running water, heated soil to replicate tropical conditions and so many other things planned; in its way it was just as fascinating as scooping.

Derek was so filled with enthusiasm at his farm, and everyone we met was clearly in awe of him. I noticed that every now and then when he had a point to emphasise, he would touch my arm. It was only the lightest touch but it sent a shiver up my arm, every time. I started to do the same and before I realised what was happening, he took my hand. It almost felt like a declaration of intent, which was fine by me. The more I was with him; the more I was thinking of him in a different way, a more serious and long-term one.

After we had been around the buildings, he looked at his watch. "Time for tea; you'll join me I hope, it's so nice to get visitors." We went back into the offices through the front entrance, still holding hands, if anyone noticed they never mentioned it and I wouldn't have cared if they had.

We sat and drank tea in his office; there were biscuits as well, which I recognised from the café. They were the ones that Davina had asked if she could buy when I had made them.

"These are my favourite," he said. "My wife used to make them; Davina stole them and thought I didn't notice." I laughed; it was a typical family thing, a special memory.

"Davina tells me you're really looking after her," he said. "I know she's not a fantastic worker but no-one's given her much of a chance before."

"It's my pleasure," I answered. "I must admit that I've heard about what happened to you and Davina and I'm trying to help in my own way."

He smiled. "There are no secrets here, Andi. I think I said that before. Yes my wife leaving was a shock, it hurt but I suppose she had good reasons, I'm not easy to live with, and work here kept me busy, still does. She left but she never got angry with me, she was always a lady."

He drank some tea. "Anyway, that's past. I think Davina was hit harder, she never says much about it but I'm sure she misses her dearly, she's never had any explanation or contact since that day and that must hurt. I can blame my job but what can she do to rationalise what happened? All she can do is blame me. I'm glad to say that she doesn't appear to; after all she chose to stay. I couldn't take losing her as well."

For a moment he looked so sad and I thought that maybe I shouldn't have mentioned it.

"And what have you been up to?" he asked. "Davina tells me that the café is busy and that you've learned to drive a Scooper."

I described my antics with Tina and he looked genuinely interested, he certainly asked all the right questions. I neglected to mention the break-in at the café and the involvement of Davina's boyfriend, I thought that he might not know about the relationship and I didn't want to drop her in any trouble.

Then I decided it was time to do a little digging. I felt bad about it but it needed to be done.

"Derek," I said, "you told me that I could come and see you if I had any questions, we've been having an argument, Cy and me, who's more important, the miners or the farm?"

He looked at me. "That's a pretty big subject. It's common knowledge that the station is owned and run by the mining company. The farm is a subsidiary company but it's wholly owned by them; there's no 'competition', we're all one thing."

I stretched the truth a little. "OK, but the thing that started this off was a conversation we overheard in the café." That was technically true, actually we had read it in the book, it had taken place in the café and if we could have decoded the video we could have overheard it.

"That was really my wife's department, liaison between the farm and the mine."

Oh crap, this was getting worse, I was telling Derek about a conversation that his wife had had whilst bonking with someone in Cy's bedroom. Still, I'd started so I had to finish.

"So why would the miners and the farmers want to argue about who was in control of the station?"

"The miners think that they're the reason the station exists. Well it was true once but since the farm started doing more than just feeding people, with all the research it's become more important. We have the power now in the eyes of the company. Of course the farm couldn't function without the water."

"How do you mean?"

"Well, all the water for the station is mined from the rocks. It's one of the by-products. But the miners hate water mining, because under their contracts they don't get paid for it. We use a lot here, and depend on a regular supply."

Everything was connected. "So if the miners wanted to prove a point, to show who was boss, they could just stop sending you water?"

"Exactly, but they don't realise that without the water, the plants wouldn't produce the oxygen that keeps them alive. Have another biscuit."

Chapter 41

When I got back from the farm, Cy had decoded more of the book. "I've found the page with all the financial details on it," he announced as I made myself a cup of tea.

"Go on then, tell me that we're rich and that we can get the money transferred with no questions asked."

"It's not that straightforward."

"It wouldn't be, would it?" He laughed. "Our Mike had a conscience after all, the money he extorted from the things he overheard and from the liaisons he recorded, apart from the pay-offs for his own antics, it went to the women who left the station. It's all gone."

"That doesn't make sense; did he pay them to go? Do you have any names?"

Yes, there's three he mentions; Morgana, who you know about, one called Heather and one just referred to as 'the lady'. She's the one who got the most, her flight was paid for and a large amount was sent to a hospital on Mars, she must have been special, maybe she was the one who was pregnant."

"What about all the other women who Mike was involved with?"

"They're still on the station, there's a list. I recognise most of the names."

So there was a list, I didn't want to see it; I'd never be able to keep a straight face in front of them.

"Don't ever let me see that list, Cy," I warned him. "You know what I'm like, I'll blab or snigger or something and it'll be embarrassing."

"Got it," he said. "How was Derek?"

"Interesting; he showed me the delicate balance on the station, how everything really is connected up here and the reason that Mike was so desperate to know what was going on."

Cy stared at me, like I was some sort of fruit cake.

"What?" I said.

"Come on, Andi. I said you'd changed, can you hear yourself?"

"What?"

"The delicate balance of the station," he mimicked me. "Honestly, it's just a floating knocking shop, full of crazies and misfits. We're just fitting in, fighting to keep our heads above the tide of filth."

He was so wrong, and I was closer to the truth than I had been, the last pieces were falling into place.

Chapter 42

Even though I didn't want to know, I did, if you get my meaning. All the time, since I had learnt of Mike's activities I had looked at every woman in the café, every one that I had met or passed and wondered if she had been one of them. And now that I knew that there was the definitive list, in Mike's own fair hand, it ate at my resolve until I was desperate for a look.

I didn't know where Cy kept his notes and the deciphered pages but I was gagging for him to go and play cards with the bunch from the farm so I could search for it. Like I said, I was close to the biggest secret of all.

It was all about 'the lady', in the notes, the one discussing the future of the station, and the one with the big pay-off. Derek had referred to his wife as a lady; Mike had said that the lady was the liaison. When she was being filmed she must have been bargaining for the station's future in secret meetings in here. She was doing what she had to so that her husband's work could continue.

Cy was off for cards, followed by home brew. "I might be going to the gym first," he said, waving his sports bag around.

"Don't you dare put your sweaty gym gear in the washer with the tea towels," I reminded him, we didn't want to fail a hygiene inspection.

"See you later," he called and left me on my own. I closed the shutters and the door, gave him five minutes and started my search.

Three hours later I still hadn't found the book, or his notes, or anything to do with it. I didn't know whether to be pleased that he'd hidden it so well or annoyed that I couldn't find it. I needed to confirm what I had remembered.

When he surfaced the next day, I tackled him. "OK, where have you hidden it?"

He smirked. "I thought you didn't want to know! I'm only protecting you from yourself, Andi."

Maz called me over to the counter. "Andi, someone here wants to see you."

It was one of Munro's burly henchmen.

"Miss Pett?" he asked. "I have a message for you. Mr Munro would like to see you. Is it alright if he comes by this evening after you've closed up?"

"What's it about, why couldn't he come here now and see me?"

The man smiled. "I'm not in Mr Munro's confidence, I just do what he tells me and I've done that, what shall I tell him?"

"Tell him that's fine but to come alone, after the break-ins we've had…" he gave a sickly grin, "…security have told me I should keep the shutters down when I'm closed up for the night, just press the intercom and I'll let him in."

Had Munro got wind of the fact that we had found the book, or had someone else and he'd found out from them? Or had he learnt about Mrs Munro's little indiscretions? The fact that he wanted to see me after hours was a worry, Cy was going to see his new mates but agreed to hang around and keep an eye.

"Mind you," he said, "if he has those two with him I might not be much use to you. You'd better have the straighteners on standby."

We shut up as normal and I got on with my jobs, one ear listening for the buzz of the intercom. As I set up for the next morning's breakfasts I heard the shutters rattle. Cy was in his room, working on the pages. My hands were full and I had stuff about to come out of the oven. "Can you go and let him in," I shouted. Predictably, there was no answer. The rattling continued.

"Cy, answer the bloody door!"

Still nothing, I lifted the trays out of the oven and ran to the door; by the time I got there the rattling had stopped. I pushed the button. The shutters didn't budge. I pushed again and they lifted slowly, then they stopped. The motor whined. There was a thump as something heavy hit the deck. The shutters, relieved of whatever had jammed them, continued their rise.

I opened the door and saw what had blocked the shutters' motion. Mr Munro had arrived. And he was very dead. I screamed.

My first thought was that I must have killed him by opening the shutters, had he got caught in the mesh somehow? I looked at his body, and at the ground. There was no blood. His eyes bulged out of his face, his mouth was open and his expression was one of silent, frightening pleading. A bit like Mike's. He must have been strangled, right here outside my café. There was grease on his sleeve where it had got tangled in the shutters. He had been dead before I had started the motor. I felt relief, then sadness. Cy joined me as I felt for a pulse, there was none but his skin was still warm.

"Who did this? And what did Munro want?"

"Call the guards, Cy," I said feeling through Munro's pockets.

"Stop, Andi," he said. "You might incriminate yourself, putting fingerprints all over." I showed him my hands; I had been wearing gloves when I rushed to the door.

"Yes, yes," he nodded. "So there's flour all over him as well." He flounced off, muttering.

There was nothing in his pockets anyway and the guards soon turned up. The first thing I did was admit that I had touched the body; I thought that would be a good plan to front up.

"Why was Mr Munro coming to see you?" one of the guards asked me, the same one I had seen so often that we could be sharing holiday snaps anytime soon.

At least I could answer that one honestly. "I don't know. One of his," I was about to say henchmen, but changed it, "team came to see me this afternoon, and told me. I asked him why and he said that he didn't know, just that it was important."

"We'd like to take a look around your café," said the one with the most braid on his jacket. "There seems to be a lot going on since you took over and perhaps it's time we tried to find out why you're such a centre of attention."

This time I wouldn't be able to put them off searching. "Come in," I sighed.

They turned the place over, paying special attention to the bedrooms. Cy had whipped out my flight folder and disguised Mike's book and his notes in amongst the paperwork, which was quick thinking. The senior guard picked at the pile strewn across his desk. "You learning to be a Scooper pilot then?" he asked Cy. "I thought I'd have a go, after all if she," he waved his hand at me, "can do it, why can't I?"

I'd make him suffer for that later, they laughed together and I could see the method in his actions, he had distracted the guard and he never looked at the papers again. That just left the freezer to worry about. I unlocked it, they opened it and rummaged and I decided it was my turn to distract them. I waited until they started removing boxes and struck. "Don't you disturb the stock rotation," I said. "You move those layers of paper and I'll be most upset."

The junior guard went red. "Sorry, Ma'am," he stuttered. He looked at the box he was holding. "These burgers are three years old. They've been here longer than I have."

I held my breath. One layer of green paper and he was into body bag territory. His boss arrived and saw the pile of boxes. "What are you up to, Simon?"

"These burgers have been in here three years, boss," he replied.

"Well get them back in there, and tidily, I don't suppose Munro was strangled over a three-year-old burger."

Chapter 43

Next morning, everyone was full of the excitement caused by Munro's death and the involvement of the café. Predictably they all thought that it had to do with Mike's book, that was the thing that everyone was talking about, again. Tina might have said it was off the menu but Munro's death had reminded everyone about the café's past. People were linking Mike with Munro's death, talking about Mike's disappearance and Heynrik and everything else that had ever happened, or at least that's how it sounded as I eavesdropped furiously.

When you said it all at once, a lot had happened since I had arrived. To the customers I must have seemed to be at least as interesting as Mike. And I hadn't really done any of the snooping that I had intended to do, goodness knows what would have happened if I had put my mind to being a detective. And what would happen if anyone ever got to hear that we had actually deciphered the book?

Davina arrived later than usual. She marched straight over to me, in full surly Goth mode.

"You've been to see my dad," she said.

"Yes, he said that I could go and see him anytime when I first met him; so did you, remember?"

"That was ages ago, why the sudden interest?" Did she mean after Heynrik? Let her ask me if that was what she wondered.

"It seemed rude not to go back and say hello. Anyway, I gave him an idea for a fish tank and I wanted to ask if it had been any use."

"Oh!" she seemed surprised that I might have an idea. "So that was you?"

Davina looked at me; she suddenly grabbed my arm, her grip like a vice. "Don't you hurt him, will you?" She had stopped being an inquisitor and become a worried daughter who loved her dad.

"Of course not." I tried to pull away but she held me firm. "Why would I do that? I really like him." She let go when I said that. I rubbed my arm, she must work out.

"Because he's upset and trusting. He likes you too, even when he had only met you once he talked about you all the time. He asks me what you've been up to every evening. Just promise me you'll look after him when I'm gone." She was pleading with me now.

"What on earth are you on about, where are you going?"

She changed the subject. "Gordie was the one caught breaking in here wasn't he?"

"Yes," I confirmed. "I'm sorry. Maz told me he was your boyfriend, and that he works for Munro. I didn't tell your dad." She was mercurial; it was hard to keep up with her moods. Now she was angry.

"He should never have put you in danger or scared you like that. I told him, you won't impress Munro by running around just cos you think it's what he wants."

"And now he's being deported?"

"Yes," she was almost crying. "I can't believe all that's happened since you turned up."

"You don't need to remind me." I couldn't believe it either. I wondered then if she meant that she was going to leave; to go to Mars for Gordie's trial. That would explain the 'look after him when I'm gone'. And there were other things for her on Mars, her mother and her half-sibling. Had I made it possible for her to leave by befriending her father?

I never got a chance to ask, she suddenly turned and headed towards the store. "I'm not here," she said as she went. I looked at the door, Munro's men had arrived.

"Is Davina here?" one asked, no preliminaries, no good mornings.

"I haven't seen her," I replied. "I'm sorry that your boss is dead, do you want me to tell Davina that you're looking for her when I see her?"

"When does she start work?" the other asked.

"After lunch," I told him.

"We'll be back then." They turned and left.

I found Davina hiding in the store; she was right in the back by the dusty 'L'. "Why do they want you?"

She shook her head. "I can't tell you, you wouldn't understand and they won't listen. You have to hide me."

"Why, what are you involved in, Davina?"

"You don't need to know. Just help me, please."

I gave her one of my spare boiler suits and one of the blue caps that I had found in a box in the store, leftovers from a beer promotion. She grimaced when she saw what I wanted her to wear. "No way," she said. "I'm not wearing that cap."

"Fine, if you don't want my help, go. But if you tuck your hair under it and pull it down, with the boiler suit on as well, no-one will recognise you."

As we were about to walk out she saw we would have to walk past Cy.

"Tell him nothing," she hissed. "We're just going for a stroll. What he doesn't know, Munro's men can't find out from him."

"Hi, Cy; me and Davina are just going for a stroll."

"Where are you off to then?" My mind raced, how could I tell him without telling him?

"Oh just where I went with Tina last week. I enjoyed it so much and Davina wants to see what was so good about it."

Davina nudged me. "That's enough."

We left; I hope he had got the message. We passed the diner on the other side, taking advantage of passing run-arounds to shield us from sight.

"Why aren't we going in the lift?" Davina asked me as we headed away from it. "There's only the secure lift down here."

"I can use it," I said. "We're heading down to the workshops.

I wanted to avoid seeing Munro's men. We're going to see Tina. She'll know somewhere you can hide down there."

But before we arrived, Davina hit the stop button on the lift. She pulled out one of my kitchen knives and started waving it around.

"What's going on, Davina?" I was scared, the knife was close to my face and I shrank back into the corner of the lift.

"I don't want to hurt you," she said, "because you're the only one who's helped me, since Mum went."

"Then why wave a knife at me? Come on, Davina, we're friends aren't we, I'll help you without all the knife waving."

She put the knife away, slid it up her sleeve. "OK, but remember it's there. You're going to take me out on a Scooper."

"Is that all, Davina? I'm licensed, I can take anyone out, anytime, you don't need to threaten me; you just need to ask."

"Oh!" She gasped. "I never realised. I'm sorry; please can you take me out on a Scooper right now." The tone was heavy sarcasm, what was going on?

"I have to see Tina first, just get her permission."

She shook her head. "No, she might not let us."

"She will, it's just a safety thing. You've been out before haven't you? Someone always has to know when you go, so if you don't come back they can raise the alarm."

She shook her head again. "I don't know anything about Scoopers," she said. "I've never been on one, we came on the shuttle; you do the talking and no funny business."

We arrived on Tina's deck and made our way over to her workbench. I suddenly wondered if she might have been in her office but she was there.

"Hi, Andi, Davina; what brings you down here?"

"Hi, Tina. I was wondering if I could take Davina out in Scooper 1? She's never been out and it'd be a treat for her." I tried to sound convincing.

"Scooper 1? OK, sure if that's what you want, just make sure you both strap in and follow all the procedures like I showed you." She had caught on a lot quicker than Cy.

"Come on," said Davina, pulling at my arm. "I'm so excited I can't wait. Thanks, Tina."

We got back in the lift and descended to the hangar. The door opened on a deserted bay, the familiar lines of craft.

"I've never been down here before," said Davina. "When you said you were qualified and allowed to fly, it was like a message. She'll help me, I thought, she'll know what to do."

"So why the knife?"

"You're right," she said, she took it out of her sleeve and threw it on the floor. "I don't need it now."

"Take this one," Davina said at the first Scooper.

"I can't do that it only has one seat," I said. "We have to take a two-seater, that's why I told Tina Scooper 1. It's the trainer."

"OK," she said reluctantly, "but no tricks."

I walked towards the Scooper on the left, trying to breathe normally.

"This one here, get in the back seat." I tried to hustle her inside before she could object. With a feeling of relief I shut the hatch behind us. I started the engine and as the Scooper rattled I turned to her.

"Strap yourself in then."

"No I'm fine like this."

"Suit yourself, it might be a bit vertigo inducing."

"I've got a strong stomach."

I went through all the checks and called Control. "Control, this is Scooper 1, I'm just going out for a practise." They answered me.

If I hadn't got into Cy's thick head, or made Tina realise that something strange was going on, perhaps the duty officer would realise that I was a qualified pilot in the simulator. And he might just put my antics up on the big screen. I lifted off and drifted towards the airlock.

"Why did you tell them that? Tina knew we were going out." She was alert again; watching as we moved across the hangar. At least she didn't have the knife. But she was sat behind me; she could reach over and hit me, grab my hair, strangle me.

"I had to, or when we left they would spot it and send a craft to investigate." It was clear that she was ignorant of procedure; she had probably never been in a small craft like this before.

"Take us out and down to the shuttle bay, hang around near it, when the Mars shuttle leaves we're going to follow it."

"What's really going on, Davina? You can tell me," I said, checking that the radio light was on. That was the last piece of the puzzle. I was pretty sure that I had worked it out, now I just needed her to confirm it, for the record. Kick back on this, Don, I thought as the meter read zero and the door opened.

Chapter 44

I called Control and drove Scooper 1 out of the station, dropping down with that gut-wrenching swoop that had me so excited when I first saw it. Davina never flinched but I felt her knees push into the back of the seat. I levelled out about five hundred metres from the shuttle bay, Scooper 1 hung in space, poised.

"It's a long story," Davina said, "but we have a while till the shuttle leaves so I'll tell you. My mum left us; I know that Dad thinks it was cos of the hours that he worked. I knew the truth but he was so upset that I couldn't tell him." She took a deep breath.

"A day or so before she went, I was cleaning Mike's rooms and I saw the famous book, there was a sheet of paper by it; he was clearly writing something to do with my mother, her name was at the top of the sheet, on one of those stick-on notes. I left it; I didn't tell Mike that I'd seen it. When I got home I asked her about it and she said that I must never tell Dad, but she had to go away. She said that she'd been to the doctor and he'd found that she was pregnant and that she had to leave the station. And that she'd been silly and now she had to pay. And that Dad must never know."

I was right so far; Mike's reference to 'the lady' had meant Davina's mother.

"And you killed Mike?"

"I was so angry, he'd split my parents up for what, a shag! My mum never let on what she was going to do and I had promised that I wouldn't say. She was in a state and just went while we were both at work. It tore me up; pretending that I didn't know what was going on.

"Sure I killed him, I pretended to seduce him, he was excited, 'the mother and the daughter, I can compare', he said. I put on my best performance, I wore him out and after when he was asleep I strangled him. He kicked a bit but I didn't care. I was getting revenge. I had a shower, scrubbed him off me, dumped him in the freezer and never told anyone."

How could I tell her that it might not have been Mike that had got her pregnant, that it could have been someone who we hadn't identified yet, and that it was all to do with saving the station and her father's work? Her mother had been protecting her father, in the only way she could. She was in a state as it was, finding that out could drive her to kill again. And this time it would be me getting strangled; before anyone could help me.

"And what about Munro, did you kill him too?" I needed the rest of the story; that must be what my rescuers were waiting for.

"Munro had his suspicions but could never pin anything on me. Gordie was my boyfriend, but Munro talked him into working for him, he told me that Munro was on about Mike's book; Munro thought that it didn't exist, that Mike had just made it up. I opened my mouth and said that I'd seen it. Gordie told Munro and he asked if he would get it.

"We had a big row, I didn't want him to get the book, he would give it to Munro and it would all come out about Mum and that would ruin Dad. Gordie wouldn't listen though; he was going to do it. God knows what Munro had promised him, then he came back with his arm all burnt; was that you?"

"Yes; I thought he was a thief or a rapist." It crossed my mind that she might be really pissed off with me, she never moved.

"Good, I told him that I hoped it hurt, and that he should leave it alone; that he wasn't to frighten you. I reckoned that if I could ask you nicely you'd help me. I'd seen the effect meeting you had on Dad. But Munro made him have another go. He got caught." She paused.

"And Munro came to see me," I said. "He told me that he was being deported on the shuttle."

"That's what we're here waiting for," she said. One more piece to go.

"So you killed Munro."

"He had taken Gordie from me, just like Mike had taken Mum. So yes, I overheard Munro's man talking to you; I knew that he was coming to see you so I followed him. In the alleyway it was easy to sneak up on him, he'd left his men at the diner and there was no-one else around. Pity you got the lights fixed, it would have been safer in the dark but I got away with it."

"Why are we waiting for the shuttle?" Surely the control room had heard enough, wouldn't they come and rescue me soon? I knew that this would all be on tape, by now Cy should have gone up to the control room for another laugh at my antics. This was one conversation he needed to hear live. My life depended on it.

"We're going to rescue Gordie, and head for Mars." She said it matter of fact, as if it would be easy. She was definitely not thinking straight, the shuttle was *going* to Mars; all she had to do was follow it.

"That's crazy."

"I know, we're on plan B, I was going to take the next shuttle. Munro's men turning up panicked me."

"How are you going to get Gordie off the shuttle?"

"I've had an idea for that; you're going to persuade them for me."

"How am I going to do that?"

"We're going to have a breakdown and they'll let us dock to rescue us. We'll be too far from the station for them to come and help, they'll have to."

She had neglected one point in her plan; the Scooper had no docking port.

"Where are they? Are you sure that radio's on?" She looked at her watch again. "They should have left by now." Ahead, the shuttle hadn't moved.

There was a knock on the hatch.

"What's that?" She was alert, her knees in the back of my seat twitched.

"Maybe it was a meteorite." I leant over, as far away from her as I could and popped the hatch. She saw my movement and froze.

"What are you doing? Are you crazy?" The hatch swung open.

Two security guards were framed by the open hatch. I knew that we were still in the hangar but Davina didn't. I had gambled that she wouldn't recognise the significance of the Scooper I had chosen. And the realism of the simulator. And I had been right.

"Wha...!" shouted Davina. I ducked and the Taser fired. The electrodes hit her square in the chest and she looked at them in shock, there was a crackle and she jerked like a harpooned fish. Then she lay still, her eyes wide open and surprise all over her face.

Chapter 45

"That was a nice job, Andi. Very cool thinking."

Cy and I were sitting in the empty café, after a very hectic twenty-four hours we were the only occupants. Everyone else had gone and it was time to relax.

"Thanks, Cy. I was hoping you'd take the hint and go up for a look."

"I wouldn't have missed it for anything, I was hoping for another anguished scream. As it happens though, it looks like we got the full story."

The news of Davina's confession was all over the station, almost before I had returned to the café. When I walked back in, with four guards, the place was full, standing room only. One of the big screens, which I'd never bothered to turn on, was playing it on a loop, the view from the cameras through the Scooper's port as realistic as it had seemed to her. The guards cleared everyone out and locked the door. While we were interrogated by a senior man, they made another full and comprehensive search of the place. This time they actually looked in the bottom of the freezer.

The senior guard asked us all about the events since we had arrived. We didn't know if he was implicated in the book or not and quite frankly I didn't care any more. I was waiting for one of the searchers to brandish it but it never happened.

I told him that we had found the body and decided to keep quiet until we knew the lie of the land, then as time passed we had been frightened into silence by Munro. I didn't want to implicate anyone else and thought that if I laid it all on him, with his reputation it might get us a bit of leeway. Cy saw where I was going and joined in. We both apologised for being stupid. He said nothing. One of the other guards came over. "We're ready to move the body," he said.

"Carry on," he replied, turning back to us as the man departed.

"So when did you suspect Davina?" he asked. Now that was tricky, without revealing the contents of the book I couldn't tell him. It was really a combination of a lot of little things.

Cy came to my rescue. "She pestered Andi for a job, she seemed desperate to get into the bedrooms and the store, she must have been looking for something."

The body was taken past us, on a trolley, they had covered it in a proper body bag and the face was no longer visible. When the guards opened the door a crowd still stood outside. A few of the women threw flowers onto the body bag as it was wheeled away.

"We've nearly finished," another guard said to our interrogator. "We found a camera in the store, hidden in a flour sack."

"Thank you, bag it up. Any books?"

"No, sir. Just the camera so far, we haven't got many more places it could be."

"Carry on then," he saluted the guard who then left. "Go on," he instructed.

"Yesterday, after Munro died, Davina was in here when Munro's men came looking for her. She was in a state and asked me to hide her from them. I said I would and then, in the lift, she pulled a knife and made me take her to the Scoopers."

"We have the knife," he said. "Go on."

"I thought that if I took her into the simulator, I could pretend to do what she wanted, that whatever she said would be heard in the control room and I would be rescued."

He nodded. "That all sounds logical, and very clever, well done, you must have been frightened but you kept your head."

I basked in his compliment. Yes, I thought, I had been clever; it was nice to have it recognised.

"Now then, this fabled book," he said. "I don't suppose you've seen it?" He looked at us.

"No, I haven't," I said, hoping I wasn't going too red. Why hadn't they found it?

"Well," he inspected his fingers, "it seems you're in the clear," he paused, "mostly. You should have reported the body to us as soon as you found it, but given Mr Munro's reputation I can understand your reluctance."

Cy and I exchanged glances.

"However," he said, "I'm not convinced that you're telling me the whole story. And after searching, twice I believe, we have found no trace of any book."

"Perhaps it really doesn't exist," I said innocently. "If you could tell everyone that's the official opinion, I might get fewer visitors in the night."

"I will have to fine you for the illicit alcohol that we found," he said.

"That was here when we moved in," Cy told him. I knew that he had got it from the farm, from his card school, but the guard seemed to accept his story.

Perhaps now we could actually get our lives back in some sort of order. The guards left, taking the bottles and the camera with them, it was a good job we hadn't found it. Our prints wouldn't be on it.

I mentioned the non-discovery of the book to Cy. It had been puzzling me.

"The book, Cy; where is it?"

"I've been keeping it in my gym bag, all the scanned pages, the memory cards, everything."

"And where's your bag? Have you left it at the gym?"

"Are you kidding, they're a thieving bunch up there and the lockers can be opened far too easily, Greg showed me. Maz has it; after Munro turned up dead and we got searched I gave it to her, asked her to look after it just in case."

"Weren't you worried that she'd look inside?"

"No, I told her it was personal stuff. She's a teacher, they might be tricky but you can trust them. Even if she looked, all she'd see, apart from my sweaty gym clothes, is the folder you kept all your flying papers in, I switched the contents."

"Tell her to get rid of it."

"I will, when we open up tomorrow."

"I have to go and see Derek." I wasn't looking forward to that, but I was sure we could work something out, I had a feeling I had plenty of time to make things right.

Hang on a minute. "Who's Greg?"

Cy smiled, he had that look of contentment. "Mind your own!"

THE END... FOR NOW!

Andorra Pett will be back soon in a brand new adventure

Here's a sample.

What was I doing here? Not for the first time I wondered that as I faced the man who had changed my life in so many ways. He had cheated on me, and I was now pretty sure that he had been responsible for the death of my oldest friend. And for what? The usual of course, money! Oh, and to try and save his own miserable neck.

The gun was pointed at me, this was it, where was my backup? I was in urgent need of a knight on a white charger; failing that, Cy would do, just as long as he got me out of here pronto! And where the hell had he got to?

In case you hadn't guessed it by now, bloody Trevor had come back into my life in the worst possible way and I hadn't felt able to refuse his sob story. And now here I was back on Mars, a place that I thought I'd left behind me. I was only here because Trevor had made me think that I had to help, that to refuse would leave me feeling guilty forever. But as I made sense of things, I realised that I had been deceived. Now it looked like I was going to pay for that misplaced loyalty.

Life in the Oort Cloud Café had settled into a pattern once all the excitement had died down and I had exorcised the past. Maz had the book, although she didn't know it, and I had no intention of looking at it. The café was doing well and the atmosphere on the station had improved now that it had never existed as far as everyone was concerned.

I had done my extra hours training and was now a fully qualified Scooper pilot; I went out every now and again and did a shift to keep my hand in and cover the miners' leave. Cy had even come out with me for a spot of sightseeing. I had started suit training as well, Tina had talked me into it and after the initial fear it felt very liberating to bob around, I could even do a few maintenance tasks, under supervision.

Even better than any of my other achievements, I had finally got off with Derek! We were officially an item, we were happy together and my life was good. I spent a lot of time at his house on the lower farm level and just used the café as a place to work. It was great to wake up to the sound of birds and the smells of the country. There weren't that many people in the solar system who could say that these days.

And then it happened. I might have guessed it, things were all working out, a sure sign that a big boot would come and kick me on the arse.

It was Cy who spotted him, I was in the kitchen chatting with Clarissa, it was pie-making day and I was engaged in a little quality control when he came in looking worried.

"Andi," he said, "don't react but there's someone out there you might not want to see."

I crammed the last of the fruit tart into my mouth and chewed. Then I went to the serving hatch and peered through; my stomach lurched and my head spun. Oh bloody hell; that was all I needed. Just when I was getting on so well with Derek, a big slice of my past had turned up. The worst thing was that just the sight of him still made me come over all unnecessary. I felt a tingle; my face must have gone red.

"Tell him I'm not here," I said to Cy, "and for goodness' sake get rid of him."

Too late, he walked in; Maz must have told him where I was. Thanks for that!

"Looks like you can tell him yourself," Cy said dryly.

"Hi, Andi," he shuffled about, keeping his distance, wise move. I tried to look him straight in the eye but he was looking anywhere but at me.

"I'm glad to see you," he said, he sounded tired.

"I'll be off then," said Clarissa, sensing the tension that had come into the room with him. She left her stuff on the counter in her haste to leave, Trevor cast an approving eye at her rear as she departed, he hadn't changed that much since I had seen him last then.

It was always either love or hate with me and Trevor; for a long time it had been hate.

"Go away," I said, "I'm over you, just like you were all over Maisie."

"Ouch! Fair enough. But honestly, I've only come here because I have nowhere else to turn." He had switched on the charm, big eyes and sad face, like a puppy caught next to a puddle.

I didn't believe him; not for a moment. "Why, has she thrown you out?" I asked as sarcastically as I could. "Caught you at it like I did?"

"It's not that," he whined. "I need your help."

That still didn't cut any ice with me, I was just getting started. "Why should I help you? What about madam fluff doing a bit? Surely she's been very accommodating so far."

"Listen, Andi, I understand, I shouldn't be here. I'm a shit and I treated you badly."

That could win a prize for understatement. I was just about to give him some more when I stopped.

His shoulders were shaking and he started to cry. "Maisie's dead, nearly a fortnight ago," he gasped.

My world stopped turning, I might have fallen out with Maisie when Trevor left me for her but I'd grown up with her, we had history, we'd been friends since our first day in primary school. We'd faced life together and rather prophetically as it turned out, we had always shared everything. Underneath it all, you couldn't change the memories of the good times. She couldn't be gone. I felt numb and sick at the same time. Beside me Cy looked like he had been hit by something heavy, his shoulders were slumped and he was welling up too.

"She can't be dead! What's happened, Trevor?" I grabbed him and shook him, and then I just held him, burying my head in his shirt front and making it very wet with my tears.

"That's why I need your help," Trevor said into my shoulder. "The police say that it was suicide but I know, I just know that it wasn't."

Bastard! He'd got me in the one place that could still override my desire to rip his bits off, my caring nature; and I knew that she would have done it for me. But underneath the grief I was still on hate. And Maisie had been the least likely person to have killed herself, what had changed, apart from the obvious? I pulled away and stood back.

"You'd better tell me all about it."

"Have you got a spare room, can I stop here?" That was pushing it a bit; the trouble was, despite everything that had happened, I was still a little bit tempted. Maybe I still loved him; maybe I was just being stupid. And I was sure that he knew what he was doing, the way he looked and the way he had fed me the story gave it away. Our relationship was all part of my past; I would have to be strong, show him that I didn't need or want him anymore.

"No you can't, there's a hostel for visitors, see the admin office." We had a spare room but I wasn't having him too close, and I would have to keep him away from Derek until I could explain; how could my life get more complicated?

Cy rolled his eyes and gave a despairing sigh, he could see where this was going, the same as I could, I was getting sucked in to Trevor's drama because, in the end, I owed it to my friend more than I did to him.

He was just the bringer of bad tidings; there was always a chance that he might have made her do it and if I found that he had I would take great pleasure in hanging him out to dry. Never mind shoot the messenger, I would do worse than that. And suicide was just so out of character, what had happened in Maisie's life?

"You could have called me before you turned up! I'm not going all the way back to Earth," I said. "I've got a café to run and I'm making a life here."

By leaving it a fortnight he had done me out of going to a funeral and grieving properly. I would have gone, despite everything.

"Listen, Andi, I know I was stupid, and it kills me every day but I really would appreciate your help."

Good, he was grovelling! I thought about it for a while as he squirmed.

"Alright; but never forget, I'm doing it because of her, not for you."

"Thank you," he said, "and you won't have to go back to Earth, this all happened on Mars."

Mars; at least it was neutral territory. "Tell me what happened."

"Maisie went to work like usual, nobody knows why but she took a vehicle and went outside."

I knew Mars had a city underground in the mountains around Tharsis; a honeycomb of tunnels had been sealed and turned into a city. There were also a few small scientific and prospecting settlements under plastic domes on the outside; I had been to Tharsis with Cy on the way to here. I couldn't say I'd enjoyed it that much, it felt artificial being underground all the time. But that was so close to leaving Earth, now being closed in didn't bother me at all.

"So what were you doing on Mars?"

"We had jobs, I worked in software and she got a job looking after the old people that had settled." That sounded a bit improbable, surely all that money hadn't been spent exploring and colonising the red planet just to turn it into a home for pensioners?

"Mars is an old folks' home?" Cy said what I'd been thinking.

"Oh yeah, they love it, the lower gravity and the sealed environment make them feel ten years younger."

I hadn't thought of that but I guess it made sense.

"Anyhow I went off to work like usual, and then I got a call asking why she hadn't turned up for her shift. I called the police; the next thing I know her vehicle has been found outside, empty; her body was found nearby."

"How did she get outside, did nobody spot her at the airlocks?"

"She went out through an old one, unmanned, that's why they reckoned it was suicide, and she was found with her suit oxygen tanks empty. She had overdosed on some sort of drug, they said, just driven out, taken the tablets and gone to sleep."

"Did she have any enemies, anyone who might want to hurt her?"

"The police asked me all this, I can't think of anyone but she wasn't unhappy, we were having a great time."

Alright, there was no need to rub it in and tell me how wonderful his life was without me. If it were true, it certainly made the verdict strange; I could sort of understand where Trevor was coming from. But I still didn't want to go, it was too late, I had needed to be there for the funeral.

"Please, Andi; come with me and just have a look around, you'll spot things that I'd miss. And you've got a reputation now; you were all over the news when you caught that murderer."

Now he was appealing to my vanity, I had been rather clever though, it was good to know it had been spotted. Perhaps I could make some outrageous demands that would put him off.

"I'm not coming without Cy, and you're paying for the shuttle for us, both ways."

He looked annoyed. "No, just you, I don't want him hanging around." Cy kept his face impassive but I could tell by the way his ears had gone red that old antagonism had been stirred up. It was time to up the ante, see what cards Trevor was holding.

"We both come or you can forget the whole thing," I said. Cy looked at me and shook his head.

It turned out that Trevor wasn't holding any cards; he really must have been desperate. "OK that's fine, I'll set it all up."

This wasn't working, try harder! I turned the knife. "And I want a hotel, a decent one, full board."

"I thought you could stay at mine," he said innocently.

Cy saved my wavering. "Well you thought wrong, if I'm coming I don't want to doss in your place, I want a hotel." Bless him; at least he was still looking out for me, saving me from myself.

Trevor threw his hands up in despair. "Alright, whatever; the shuttle will be leaving tomorrow."

Hang on a minute! That was a bit quick, I hadn't thought he would go for the expense of taking both of us, it wasn't like Trevor to have money to throw around, he must be serious.

"Tomorrow?" I panicked. "I can't just get on a shuttle tomorrow, I have responsibilities, there's one every week, what's the rush?"

"Please, Andi. It's taken me a week to get here, and it'll be another one to get back. I had to wait for the investigation to get a verdict, you said you'd come and there's no time to waste."

Put like that it was reasonable but why did I get the feeling that I was being rushed? Surely he could have called me from Mars, or even while he was on the way and we could have talked it over. Trevor had some other agenda; he hadn't mentioned any urgency until I'd agreed to help.

"Pack your bags, I'll go and sort the tickets out. I'll see you at the departure gate in the morning." He rushed out; clearly he had forgotten all about staying in the café. I felt exhausted and numbed by his company and his news. Cy went off muttering, it wasn't just me and Derek, we both had reasons to stay. I finished up the day's work in a bit of a daze.

"Who was that?" asked Maz while we were closing up. "I hope I did right letting him in, he said he knew you and that it was important."

Maz, she was my rock in the café; she had lived on Mars for years, taught school there and knew more about it than I did, I'd only been there a few months, hardly long enough to notice anything about how the place worked. Anything she could have told me would have been worth it, if only I'd have had the time to ask her.

"That," Cy said grandly, "was Trevor, Andi's ex and the reason we ended up here. And now he's talked her into going off to Mars!" He shook his head. "And I'll have to go and hold her bloody hand, or who knows what'll happen."

Six months ago, he would have been a lot less charitable, initially he hadn't wanted to be here, never mind want to stay long term. Events and Greg had persuaded him otherwise.

"He seemed upset." She had spotted that straight off. "Did you say that you're going to Mars?"

"I'm sorry about the short notice, Maz. I need to ask you if you'll manage the café for us. Like Cy says, Trevor needs us to go to Mars for a while. I don't know how long I'll be gone but he needs our help." I wasn't more specific than that, if I tried to explain we would be here all night, and I had things to do.

She took it all in her stride, just like the teacher she had been. "Of course I will, I'll tell everyone; don't you worry about the café. You go and help your friend."

Andorra Pett on Mars will be published in 2018.

Keep up to date with the latest from Richard Dee at

www.richarddeescifi.co.uk

Lightning Source UK Ltd.
Milton Keynes UK
UKHW010643070421
381585UK00001B/126